the god thing

Serial fiction, once popularised by Dickens, is being revived online. Nada Holland, pioneering the form anew, loves the instant rapport with the reader, and the possibilities of making a story happen in real time. It's more like TV, or radio, she thinks, than like books.

Nada Holland is a former newspaper editor. She wasn't much good at reporting, finding she preferred stories to facts. After writing her first novel, *Amerika*, in 2009, she didn't quite feel she'd cut it as a novelist either, feeling half demented with isolation and frustration at her own relentless rewrites.

the god thing therefore started out as very short fiction, published on a blog. It grew into a series.

This volume collects the first two seasons. It's not a novel, and it's not a short story collection. It's more raw, a story finding its feet in a new medium. It doesn't strive for perfection, capturing instead, perhaps, a new moment in fiction. Like TV, it grows organically, wearing its continuity errors, its beginner's mistakes, its imperfections on its sleeve.
Consider this the box set.

Then go catch up online.

ISBN 978-1-4457-9935-3

Copyright Nada Holland 2011
Photos Petra Droogsma
Edited by Ruth Clarke
Cover Ananda Holland and Nada Holland

Published by *bam*books London 2011

the god thing

nada holland

For Omar, of course.

Love and violence—not to conquer one with the other but to live with both, that's what I've learned. Each pulling me a different way. If I relax my struggles they don't tear me in two, but lift me up.

— Denis Johnson

1

rapture

She's in the window. Reaches up to close a blind. The walls are black.
Her shape is a cut against the pale blue curtain.
The voice of Anita Baker fades away on YouTube, the song still heavy in the room.

Omar watches as she shrugs off, back still turned, a fluffy cardigan. It falls away from her in halves, leaving straight, thin shoulders. She drops a pleated skirt, steps out and turns to face him.
He lifts her onto the bed.

Through the pale blue curtain, a prayer call drifts into the room. A truck rattles in the lane. Inside the black walls, on the black covers of the bed, her body glows. He cannot read her. She is a foreign face, encrypted, in a distant language, an alien script. It's not her paleness. He's slept with English girls. It's her. Looking at him. Nothing he sees her seeing, computes with what he knows. He doesn't know the man she's looking at. Who is he? Omar plunges in, mastering somehow the deep unknown, King of the tides--absolutely certain he is nowhere, he is lost, he is nothing.
Is he in love?

Afterwards, rattling down her stairs, he curses under his breath. He hasn't eaten since last night. It's Ramadan. He's fasting.
Omar is faint, his knees buckle, knocking into the dusty staircase. He opens the door out into the East End grime. It's Sunday. As he has every other day this week, he has slept through the pre-dawn meal of *sahur*. He is not to eat or drink again till dusk, tonight. It is the month of atonement. From *sahur,* at dawn to *iftar* at dusk, there's no smoking, no drinking, no anger. No lying or cheating, no envy or desire, no greed. He stands in the street, as the first hipsters drift about him under the Brick Lane sun, as clouds pass overhead, as from the mosque across the street bearded men step out into the road, their feet slipping back into their shoes. He's shaking. Shadows pass over girls in sunglasses and denim hot pants, over the white caps of the hajis now streaming out.

2

Omar wishes, for the moment, he'd heeded the Prophet's call, to wake in the dead of night and eat, before dawn this morning, 'For Verily, there is a blessing in *Sahur*.' He has, however, just slept till noon, then fucked his French girlfriend. Nouche.

Approaching Brady Street he pauses. Whitechapel Sainsbury's is under construction, scaffolds and scarlet tarpaulin slapping in the wind, the air pounding with pneumatic drills. He's here to shop. Omar's youngest sister, Abebech, is to visit his flat later tonight. She is now married, to a skinny boy in slippers and white socks, with a struggling bit of fluff on his chin. For verily, Omar thinks, there must be a blessing in beards. The boy will drop her off tonight, as he has been doing, occasionally, over the past few months.

Three, Omar counts. Three months.

He has now been off gear for nine months altogether, off all crack. Nine months. Enough to be renewed, reborn, he thinks, enough to be born again. Like a baby. Omar, baby brother, to Abebech, his baby sister.

A fucking rebirth, that's what he's had, he thinks, turning the corner, into Brady Street, heading for Sainsbury's side entrance. Here to get a box of cup cakes, to serve to his married sister Abebech, baby steps, left right, knees still shaking, down the stained, battered pavement. Nine months, of living indoors. Three months of seeing his sister, his mother. Of talking on the phone, a landline, not the pay-as-you-go mobile, not the public phones he only ever used to call his dealers. Three months now of sitting indoors, sipping Tetley's, and talking to his mother on the phone.

He turns the corner, baby steps, one foot in front of the other. Machines hammer like poltergeists from behind the construction boards. Omar sniffs the air, spiked with burnt plastic and newspaper. Half pushed into the corner of the scaffold, a low tent crouches on the pavement. A toothless face waits by the small fire of plastic bottles and paper cartons. A beer can, cut open, blisters on the flames.

Omar passes the tent. He is mouthing his shopping list, *cake, milk, matches*. He passes the bearded bunch of rags bent over the flames. Jimmy. It's Jimmy.

Omar reaches in his pocket, and lays a coin in Jimmy's palm. *Ariel*, he thinks. He's out of detergent. He presses Jimmy's hand, and moves on, away from the poky fire, the beer can, the charred casserole bubbling angrily inside. *Allah*, he's hungry.

At the supermarket entrance, he hesitates. He could quickly run around the corner and nip into the library. Oops, the *Idea Store*. The Tower Hamlets Whitechapel Library is now the Idea Store, a multi-storey green glass facade. Rumi, is what he wants, craves, suddenly, more than caramel cupcakes. Rumi, the Persian poet, the Sufi master of rhythm and rhyme.

The way I look is so fragile,
yet here in my hand
is an assurance of eternity.

He's glad to see there are new guards at the door. He passes the metal detector gates, still grateful to slip into a public building unhindered. Omar has spent the past two decades being thrown out of hostels and hospitals, banned from shops, barred from surgeries and churches. Years of lying, in convulsions, on some public doorstep. Baby steps, he thinks, tiptoeing into the hall, one foot in front of the other.

Posters on the wall of the Idea Store show the historical East End. He stops at his favourite sign, slapped across an entire Victorian facade. *Soup Kitchen For The Jewish Poor*. The doorways, just to be absolutely clear, are marked *WAY IN* and *WAY OUT*. The sign, and its language, lacks every trace of the imagination, of rhythm or rhyme. The sign is devoid of Rumi's touch, of his *The way I look is so fragile*. It is, Omar thinks, so bluntly literal it never fails to cheer him.

A shelf of *Ramadan Quick Picks* offers up Rumi right in the hallway. He presses the *Selected Poems* to his chest and continues to browse. Islamic texts sit side by side, on the neighbouring Science Year display, with the bold cover of *The God Delusion*. He picks up a copy, an audiobook, he reads, by Richard Dawkins, author of *The Selfish Gene*. Read by Lala Ward. He sets the book back on the shelf. Right, he thinks, they're married.

Omar checks out the Rumi and emerges from the gates, again, without incident. Lala Ward traded Doctor Who for Dawkins. Now there's a let down, he thinks.

He's back on the corner of Whitechapel Road. Brady Street looms in the green sheen of the library, a dark, stinking alley, more potholed than the roads of Addis under Mengistu. Lala Ward! Fallen for Richard Dawkins, the pope of militant Atheism. Only the Brits, he thinks. They are so bloody-minded, so literal, they call a library, a place of fable and rhyme, not the Well, or the Fountain, but the *Idea Store*. The French may have proclaimed God's demise, but only the Brits would call faith itself *The God Delusion*.

Nothing's changed in this place, he thinks, from the days of the *Soup Kitchen*, or *The Jewish Poor*.
Everything is literal, the land organised like a lab, named and labeled with all the imagination of a civil servant in a white coat. A sign reading *WAY IN* on one side, *SOUP/ CULTURE/ IDEA STORE* plastered across the bit in the middle, and on the other end, *WAY OUT*.

When I first arrived, he muses, turning into Brady, I used to think the Brits were just taking after the Americans, dumbing down. I was wrong, he thinks. It's the Brits who were dumb first. The Yanks are just dumb cause their lot was Brits to begin with.

On the pavement, there is a large, human turd.

I should be voting Tory, he thinks.

At least they'd hate me for having the wrong god. Labour only condoned my god because they think I'm stupid and deluded. They think it's cultural. They think I'm backward, and my faith's a delusion, but it's not my fault. It's just my *culture*.
Which, and this is the whole point of the exercise, makes them not racist for

thinking I was stupid to begin with.

It just makes me more fodder, more *Jewish Poor*, to be lined up at the *WAY IN* end, and led through the *Idea Store*.

In their haste, they manage to bypass, entirely, the fact that my stupid little culture means *surrendering to God*.

To God, he thinks. To the here, the present. To Rumi's *fragile*, to his *assurance*, his *Eternity*. The One Love.

I am surrendered, he thinks. To the East End sun, to the English clouds drifting overhead, casting their chill across Brady Street, turning the emerald glass of the Idea Store a grimy bottle green. I am surrendered even to Labour, to the Lib-Dems--New, Old, patched up, bent over backwards.

Mama, he says, dropping his shopping on the counter, and picking up the phone. *Salam mama*.

Yes, he nods. I'm fasting.

He opens the fridge and shoves in the box of cakes.

Yes, he repeats. I'm praying.

He pictures his mother, Aatifa, her high shoulders and straight back. She sits on a wood bench outside the kitchen wall, behind the tall grill fencing in a large, ground floor council flat. He imagines dropping the phone, and listening for a moment, for the clear pitch of her voice, its shrill notes carrying across the few, cloud-swept streets that separate his own council kitchen from hers.

He shakes his head. Not much news mama. I'm reading Rumi.

He takes out the Ariel and sticks it under the sink.

Nine months. A rebirth. Talking to his mother, on the phone, hearing her voice, seeing her before him, her back resting gently against the wall, her robe crisp and white among the potted plants. He nods into the phone, as she discusses her children. Abebech, his sister, and his brother, Wendimu.

He reads her Rumi.

If, for penance, you crush grapes,
you may as well drink the wine.

You imagine that the old sufis
had dark sediment in their cups.
It does not matter what you think.

He hears his mother, breathing on the other end. Go on, she says.

As everyone drifts off to sleep,
I am still staring at the stars.

His mother sighs.

Separation from you does have a cure, he reads.

There is a way inside the sealed room.

He sees black walls, black sheets, small white feet, and blushes.

If you will not pour wine,
at least allow me half a mouthful
of leftover dregs.

His mother murmurs. He can see her, too, her white dress stiff behind the
freshly painted grill of the fence; pots, flowers, dangling from its wrought iron
curls.

You need no name.
You are the ocean.
I am held in your sway.

Again, she sighs.

When I am outside you,

life is torment.

Her children number five, not three.

She's lost two. Almost as soon as it occurs to Omar, the thought is gone.
He is still sitting on the floor, under the sink; his mother on her bench outside
her own kitchen. The children, a little brother, a missing sister, even their
names, lie buried once more in the ground between them. They are gone, and
all that's left is Omar's deep, intimate knowledge of his mother's heart; and her
breathing on the other end of the line. *Rapture*, he thinks. *Surrender*.

He himself was lost to her. She may have crushed grapes for penance, he
thinks. She may dwell with sufis, drink the darkest sediment: she may
surrender, to God, drunk on the wine of rapture. But, he thinks, she has not
seen a bottle of spirit in her life. There is not a way in this world she could
comprehend the words *crack cocaine*.

Nine months, he thinks. Baby steps.

Then Solomon walks back into Jerusalem, he reads,

And a thousand lanterns illuminate.

Nine months, a fucking rebirth.

He can see his mother, behind the bars of her gate, her white robe; her children
gathered at her feet: conjured up by the sound of their names on her lips. He
presses the phone to his ear, although he could hear her breathe now not
through the line, but across the Tower Hamlets estates.

The divine glory settles
into a mountain nest.

He reads her these last lines, into the phone, but, really, just mouths them out
loud, as though speaking straight into her ear--as though being really, finally,
back in that nest--back on the other side, on the inside, of her grill fence.

Later, he climbs the stairs of the Whitechapel Detox classroom. It is dusk, past eight: time for Iftar, the opening of the fast. The meal however, blessed or not, will have to wait till after the meeting. Verily, Omar has worn his own personal grooves into these steps, which are not baby steps, he thinks, not baby steps at all, but rock-hard, granite monsters, steep, unyielding fuckers. These stairs are the kind of concrete he used to wake on, colder, less giving than the hands of hell. These are the kind of stairs he would find himself trying to go back to sleep on, the kind sitting under a battery of strip lights, like a flood-lit, concrete grotto. He's passed out on on stairs like these more times than he could rememeber, lulled by some warped sense of security, only to wake, moments later: blinded, strung out, hypothermic, and persecuted by the relentless buzz, the blaze, the overkill of the lights overhead.

He is now carrying a mug of tea up the stairs, which will have to do for Iftar, and which he deposits on the first available surface in the room. He is hailed, first by Anwar, then Marquis and Terry, a long, serial hug he receives and returns. By the end of it he is aglow, the mug forgotten on the table, then remembered, picked up, brought to his mouth. Water. It goes down like the dark dregs of the sufis. I am, he thinks again, surrendered.

You are, Terry says, a proper cunt.

It's later, the lights in the room have been turned full tilt, and Omar has just read out a four page story of his life.
It's feedback time.
Omar nods at Terry.
He looks around the room.

Marquis nods, the others too bow, in accordance, it seems, with Terry's verdict. Verily, Omar thinks, there is accordance in the room. And in accordance, he thinks, surely there's a blessing.

He closes his eyes, allowing himself to float, for the moment, on the spirit of unity, of fraternity. He looks up again, at the concrete walls of Day Centre, at the strip lights buzzing overhead, and thinks, Verily.
A cunt.

Abebech is dropped off at his front door. He shakes hands with her young husband, who heads off, his white-capped head held high, for prayers at the East End mosque.
Omar is reminded, watching the boy disappear down his tiled hallway, of a canvas, leaning against Nouche's black walls this morning. Painted after the London underground, it showed a tiled tunnel, converging in the middle. There, at the end of the passage, she had painted a single, blue square.

Watching his sister's husband patting down the hall in his slippers, the white cap on the boy's head disappearing in the centre, in the distance, he is reminded of that square.
He turns to welcome his sister.

In the kitchen, as she goes through messages on her iPhone, he pours her tea. It's been a hot day, and she has been kept waiting at the Regent Street Apple Store all afternoon, her appointment to get her phone fixed running late.

'My chicken sweating away on the kitchen counter,' she rants. Her young face is a near perfect sphere in its long veil, her small, sharp features so stark she looks modelled out of onyx.

'I'm fasting, I tell them,' she says, 'I'm fainting, and haven't even started on the bloody chicken..'

He pictures Iftar, spread out at Abebech's flat, before her youthful husband this evening, the round table covered in soft *ijera*, chicken *wat* sitting in a spotless little heap.

He is hungry, suddenly, for the first time in hours, and realises he has still not actually eaten. Caramel cupcakes then, for what is in effect breakfast, lunch and dinner. Baby food: his own, baby Iftar.
He is sure he's had worse.

In his room, white, bare apart from two straight-backed chairs and the table now bearing a platter of cakes, he watches his sister glance at a postcard he has taped to the wall, a flyer, actually, for a group show Nouche was part of. It features another of her works.

In it, she has painted Tate Modern's Turbine Hall. The outsized space, like the tunnel, is empty. Parallel lines converge in the middle, on the back wall, which too is empty, save a single box, like a blue star, right in the centre. Another framed blue square.

His sister, lifting a bite of caramel icing, peers at the painting.
''s Just like..' she says. '..The Kaaba.'
Slowly, she drops the fork and suddenly, he is an eldest brother, and she, again, his baby sister. She whispers.
'..Like Mecca.'

Abebech's eyes widen, as Nouche appears in the doorway. Thinking it was her husband, Biru, here to pick up his sister after prayers, Omar has just buzzed her in. Now he is struggling with her in the doorway, his leonine instincts having led him to both squeeze against the wall to welcome her in, and now to somehow scramble past her into the room. He is tripping over his feet in an array of conflicting urges, an erratic wildfire of gallantry which bewilders even himself.

Finally, she stands, in the middle of the room, under the bare lightbulb. Slight, almost transparent, in a silk skirt and heels. The fluffy cardigan wrapped around her shoulders. All he has to offer her is the straight-backed chair, and he is already doing so, with gusto, with both abandon and, he realises, dread, as he settles her, finally, at the small table--right opposite his sister.

Nouche is tiny but grand, somehow, a powdery, ragged elegance radiating from her. She's perfectly amiable, and his sister's stark features too, are softened with smiles. He himself however is on edge, all over the place; his instincts run riot. His young sister is solid as a house in her ankle-length robe, her veils hiding her hands down to her scrubbed pink cuticles. His girlfriend, by contrast, appears to be held in her seat by no apparent force of gravity, might be hanging on to the table solely with her long, Chanel red nails.

Abebech is back on the topic of queues in the Apple Store. She's is picking away at the caramel icing, first one cake and, as Omar stands watching, a second. Nouche would not touch a cupcake if it was the Last Supper, he thinks. She'd opt straight for the Cross, instead.

As he watches Abebech toy with the third, a feeling starts in his gut, a new, fresh dread, unnamed as yet, a new sense to contend with the array playing havoc on his nerves as it is, his raw, bare, baby nerves, *nine months old,* he thinks.

It has been nine months, at most, that he's had feelings in the first place. Not that he would have known: he has learned, the hard way, Terry's way, to identify them. Feelings: weird, seismic changes in outlook. He cannot remember having had any, ever, before. He was a mountain, an iceberg. Calm and even: unperturbed. His shipwrecks were reliable, constant, but distant, remote, occurring always on the outskirts, and, somehow, to those around him, to other people's vessels.

Now he, himself, is one of those ships. One of the wrecks, constantly running into large, submerged objects, subject himself to upheaval. Rumi, Omar thinks. *The way I look is so fragile.*

He stands by the table, faint with effort, gazing at the postcard on the wall, the painting. Surrender, he thinks, almost sinking to his knees. He is moved, suddenly, to tears, by that blue square, like a doorway, marked *WAY OUT.*

He looks at his sister, who is smiling, looks at her round cheeks, surprised to find himself still standing, on his own two feet, in his own room: not actually in a heap on the floor.

She's *pregnant*, he thinks. And she doesn't know.
Not quite. Not yet.

In the kitchen, Abebech runs a thumb across the plate and, like child, lands it in her mouth.
Again, he blushes, thinking of his girlfriend's pale legs, her feet pointing to opposite ends of her sheets, his own hand sliding in between.
His sister points at the other room and whispers in his ear, 'She's just like you. *Old.*'

Why am I always catching the end, only, of that song, he thinks, later that night, as Anita Baker dies out, again, on YouTube. Nouche is curled up on her bed, her back against the wall, staring at the unfinished canvas on the opposite end of the room. The empty glass dangles from her fingers, which lock over her knees. She is brooding, darkness emanating from her bones.

Again he is tearful, watching the deep furrow in his girlfriend's brow. She is hating her painting, he can tell. She is airless, locked into the tunnel of her discontent, her own disenchantment. *So fragile.*

He sees through her, reads her like a poem, could drink her, like her own claret, like the dark dregs of the sufis. It is *rapture* she's after.
Still, even staring at her own painting, her own blue square, her Kaaba, her own doorway marked *WAY OUT*, she fails to read, to even see, the sign.

There is no way in the world, he thinks, she could comprehend the word *Surrender*.

He picks up his Rumi, and reads, this time to her.

The blood in our bodies carries
a living luminous flow.

He aches to show her her own painting, through the eyes of the sufi, aches to tell her, *let go*. He is piling on words, a mountain of words, an iceberg, anything to jolt her boat, to show her that once she is out in the open, surrendered, she will be free.

But watch when it spills out
and soaks into the ground.

He glances around the page, frantic for the right word, the right sentence. He should write his own. He could write an entire story. *Rapture*.

He looks up at her small, intense shape, wrapped up, caught up, in her own embrace, her arms crossed before her, like two barrelled guns.
It would never work.

Omar sighs, and returns to the poem.

That is how speech does, he reads.
Overflowing from silence.

Silk on one side,
cheap, striped canvas on the other.

She yawns.

Lazily, she drops the glass, her arms, and lowers her knees, spreads them, her small white feet pointing, again, to opposite ends of the black sheet.

Omar thinks, still, a line or two, but really, they are lost. His words, his speech, like cheap, striped canvas, is fading, petering away, like Anita Baker's last notes, as he plunges, has plunged already, long since by now; has lost himself, all over, in the dark pit of her tunnel, her dead end, her bright blue star.

2

the one

Nouche makes an entrance. A childless Parisian, in stockings and heels and a fluffy cardigan sitting around her shoulders like a lazy, longhaired cat. A hand with a pearl bracelet, protectively on the maroon pouch slung across her chest. Suede tassels drip from her hip like streaks of blood. The London East End gallery is a dump.

She turns heads, until she stops at the first large canvas, or, to be more precise, at Billie Jean, its painter. Billie Jean glowers, shuffling from one sneakered foot to the other. She is slight herself, in skinny jeans and a t-shirt; still she stands before the painting like a buttress, like a warhead.

Nouche stops. Instinctively, she clasps the bag, a vintage Saint-Laurent, to her chest. It sits there like a suede heart, spilling down her front. As she grasps the pouch, her bracelet snags on the shoulder strap, and before she knows it, pearls roll out from her, on the concrete floor, and she stands there, like Cinderella in the cartoon coach, pearls running away from her like minute, white mice, stopping only at Billie Jean's sneakered feet.

Billie Jean. The canvas is huge, deliberately oversized, parodying the painterly testosterone of the fifties. A large nude is depicted, her jutting breasts cut out of paint, Willem de Kooning-style, with a knife.
It reads *SHE SAYS/*
I AM THE ONE.

Nouche, a painter herself, is now forced to sink to her knees in the gallery--an abandoned Tower Hamlets eighth floor flat--to scramble after her pearls, scattered between Billie Jean's black Converse high tops.

Ouch, Nouche cries.

She stares at her fingernail, which glitters, a sliver of metal sticking out.

'What the..'

She holds up the hand. Something has caught under her nail, straight into some nerve, causing her head to spin. She is crouched on the floor, probably cutting off the blood flow in her knees, making her dizzier yet--making her, now, for an instant, black out. She can't see.

She grasps for the floor, then, as her vision returns, without thinking, wipes her hands on a silk skirt. She brings up the aching nail, once more, and pulls out the metal, a spike, broken, *a goddamn spike,* she thinks, *a goddamn needle.*

She's sucking the finger, thinking, *great. Magnifique, so here it is, at last, le goût de Sida.*
The taste of Aids.

She looks up, where another hand is now descending, a small, unadorned hand, bare apart from a set of prison tattoos. Billie Jean. It grasps her under her armpit, and lifts her, like a doll, to her feet. Here she is, Nouche, suddenly upright, seven inches away from Billie's own chest, her small breasts and shoulders boxed into a faded black tee.

Nouche steps back, clutching her bag, and glances around, for a drink. A table in the corner is conspicuously stocked with bottled water and lemonade. *Lemonade.*

Right. Billie Jean is one of *those*, she thinks. Omar's lot. Billie Jean has that same look, raw, open nerved, wearing her bruises, her battered heart on her skin, like armour.

Nouche searches the pouch for a cigarette, lights it, and blows smoke, away from the woman before her and, accidentally, into the painting. She steps back further, still reeling in her heels. Someone appears to be handing her the pearls, and she has to clamp the cigarette between her lips, holding up both palms, and stuffing the lot into the Saint-Laurent. She looks up to find Billie Jean still standing, unruffled, before the painting, which seems to Nouche, on closer inspection, now mostly a vagina.

She smoothes down her cardigan, exhaling a long squirt of smoke, and straightens a pale skirt. *Great,* she thinks, again, staring down her front, where,

before, she'd wiped her hands, and where now a bright red stain sits nested right at her cream silk crotch. *Sida*, she thinks. *Magnifique.*
Aids á la mode.

Omar. That morning, he had got up from the bed in her black-walled flat, and descended her stairs, as usual, into the Brick Lane sun. His nappy head appeared in the street under her window, among the white caps of the slippered men spilling from the mosque across the road. She watched from the window, as he drifted away among the Sunday crowd, black sheep among the hajis. His shoulders somehow glowed, towering over the hipsters, the kids flocking down the street in silly spectacles and drainpipe jeans.

He was fasting. Ramadan. Refusing food, drink, water, refusing even to judge her, as she'd uncork a bottle at four--after staring at her own unfinished canvases through most of the afternoon. He'd read to her, instead, feeding her with words, words she did not get, sentences, images which always somehow failed in her, to connect. She'd watch his face, that glow that also, always, left her sinking, feeling somehow wanting, left her guessing, for more, *is that an expression,* she thinks.

Guessing for more.

It's later, midnight. She's on the bed, alone, in her flat. Predictably, tonight's opening, powered by lemonade, was not of the hard partying kind. She's staring at the black wall across from the bed, staring still at her own canvas stacked against it, a painting of a tunnel with a bright blue square in the middle, where the dead end wall should be.

It's the London Underground, she thinks. Or Hell. Or whatever you wanna call it, all this--Life*,* she thinks, tired, fed up, suddenly, with words altogether. *La Vie.*
She rolls down her stockings. She's on the bed, in an old french slip, the cardigan still purring around her shoulders. On the floor, her suede bag lies.

She stares at the blue square in the middle of the canvas, which is *International Klein Blue*, the transcendent blue of Yves Klein's *Monochromes*.

Yves Klein, the artist who could be seen leaping from a Paris window, swimming up in the sky smiling, like a hatchling, a baby bird, in a 1960 performance called *Le Saut dans la Vide--The Leap into the Void*.

Klein's blue squares, she broods, in her own painted tunnels, are *La Vide*--blue doorways, she thinks, to the hereafter, the afterlife, some place else--anywhere but here.

She sighs, turns from the canvas and opens a MacBook, gleaming on her black sheets.
She skims through Omar's Facebook friends. There she is.
Nouche browses her profile pictures: photo's, paintings, snapshots.

SHE'S JUST A GIRL, a painting reads, *WHO CLAIMS*

There are pictures of her in overalls, before tonight's huge canvas, the De Kooning nude, red paint, like lipstick, streaked across the pubis at the centre.

Nouche glances back at her own canvas, the bleak tunnel, the painted Underground. *There must be some kind of way out of here*, she thinks.

Said the joker to the thief.

There must be some way out of here, out of this life, whatever you call it, she thinks, swallowing the last dregs of claret; disgusted with words. There must be Some Place Else.

She stares at her own work, at the blue square in the centre, then returns to the MacBook, the Facebook album. Billie Jean, slashing words across the painting

SHE'S JUST A GIRL WHO CLAIMS THAT..

The bell rings.

It's Omar coming up the stairs, carrying another book under his arm.

Rumi, he says, as she pours herself a glass. The Sufi master.

Nouche sits brooding on the bed, holding her knees and still gazing at the canvas, the tunnel, the pure blue heart in the middle, *true blue,* she thinks.

The blood in our bodies carries, Omar is reading.
A living luminous flow.

She remembers the pictures: Billie Jean, painting the words,

..I AM THE ONE

But watch when it spills out, Omar reads.
And soaks into the ground.

Nouche rests her chin on her knees and stares into her tunnel, across from the bed. The black walls converge in the blue heart, the true heart of the painting. There is nothing *there*, she thinks suddenly, staring at her own work, and panicking. There's *nothing* there. No god. No Saviour. Nothing beside the room, the born-again boyfriend. This is *it*.

Omar lived in flats like that, like tonight's gallery, she thinks, half his life. Eighth floor flats with nothing there. Bare rooms, stripped down to the concrete floors, black tunnels full of junkies, of people curled up in themselves like balls, like infant corpses, where you'd go from wall to wall and the the only sound would be the carpet of needles splintering under your soles.

That is how speech does, Omar reads.
Overflowing from silence.

Nouche is sick with dread. How can anyone live. How can anyone live this way. There cannot be a God.

Silk on one side, Omar is saying.
Cheap, striped canvas on the other.

He lays down the book. This is it, she keeps thinking. There's nothing there. Just this room, the gentle, born again buck, his black sheep's hair glowing, always just out of reach, leading where she doubts she'll follow.

Speech wells up in her mind, just words, out of nothing, leading nowhere. *This is how he looked,* she hears herself thinking. *The Son of Man.*

No.

There's nothing here, she thinks, rebuking her own words. *No Son, no Man.*

Just this. The room, her ranting crackhead boyfriend. Her own failed canvas. Her pearls, stuffed into a Saint-Laurent pouch, crushed in a heap on the floor. She is suddenly weak with grief. She cannot love this man. May not, will not. She doesn't know him. He'll leave her behind. There's nothing here, she is alone, her heart, her future, her unborn children, that lifeless brood, scattered around her on the floor, small corpses she never even managed to conceive.

She too will die.

She'll disappear, into the Void.

She lowers her gaze from the painting, lets go of the knees. Her legs fall sideways on the bed, feet apart. She drops the glass. She says nothing. In many ways, she feels, her body is a corpse in rigor mortis, going through the motions. Void already.

Still she doesn't speak. Doesn't need to. All she did was point. Two bare feet, pointing out *la Vide* on the sheet.

21

It's Omar, who takes the plunge. Omar, who, as it turns out, loves her, all of her, but most of all those pearly, pointing toes. He is the one. He leaps for the void, like a baby, like a newborn, swimming out into the sky.

3

abstract

Sahur. Omar is in the bathroom. It's 4 in the morning, and he could eat a horse. He stares in the mirror. Has he, Omar wonders, lost weight?

Omar is large. His frame, mangled for twenty years, has filled out, like enforced concrete, poured around his bones in a cast which is like nothing he can remember. There is not a trace left of the gangly youth, the long cardboard limbs of the man who slept folded into doorways. Omar is solid, *recast*, he thinks, astonished, *in the eyes of God*.

If anything, he approaches the toddler he once was, that solid little act of will. It's true. Omar is chubby. His flesh abounds, it sits on him seemingly without effort or care. Virtuoso flesh. Unaccountable, he thinks. An act of grace.

He is heavy now. A man of gravitas. His hair has grown. He's handsome. This is so ridiculous it makes him pull a face in the mirror.

He thinks of his girlfriend. Through an opposite act, she is barely more than the sum of her bones, an extracted version of herself, an abstract: heady, wilful, like perfume.

He is erect at the thought. And hungry. It is time for sahur, the last meal of the night, before the fast, this holy month of Ramadan. He has eight minutes until dawn. There will be, Omar thinks, no lust, no anger, no food today. No stealing, he muses, no dealing, no robbing or cheating. No gear, he counts off, with relief, no crack, no smoking or drinking. Another day, another handful of negatives. Verily, he sighs, there's a blessing in *that*.

He looks down at his cock. It, too, is recast. It is nothing he can remember. It scares him. Godzilla's alive, with a passion wholly alien to him. He is now a passionate man, a man of the senses. A handsome man with a passion. It makes no sense.

He remembers trying to wank, for hours, unsuccessfully, with the crackling pages of crack house porn. Remembers, if anything, the sound of snapping syringes as someone would shuffle past behind him in the dark, in the cold, in someone else's no heat, no light flat. He remembers willing up desire for women he felt no desire for, remembers being held up solely by violence, by women splayed for his convenience, their abjection splinting his erection, spouting his ejection; snot and bile. Disgust.

If he has memories of shagging at all, it is not of the women he's been with. He remembers willing them to sleep, their nervous little breaths beside him filling him with despair. He remembers, vaguely, shagging other people's girlfriends, their hard, unattractive faces turned to the wall.

Now here he is, with a massive hard-on, thinking of a woman who, by all accounts, he considers his own. Is this normal?

Nouche. Last night, she'd sat on the bed biting a long red nail, and staring at her painting. She'd leaned back the pillows, her eyes narrowed at the canvas. Then she'd shrugged, and dropped a pale blue cardigan from her shoulders.

The painting was the London underground, the passage, with the square, like a doorway, at the end. That night, though, the tunnel, which Nouche had been working on for days, had been transformed. It was red. Glossy, shiny, a shade Omar hadn't seen before, unless perhaps, he'd thought, on a Porsche. Grand Prix, F-1, *fuck-off* red.

Sitting against the wall beside his girlfriend, Omar had recalled his first car. His first love, perhaps, he'd thought, apart from his mother. It must have been thirty years ago, in Dubai, in transit: the Haji season. He must have been on his way to Mecca. He was a toddler. Awaiting a connecting flight, sometime later that week, his mother had taken him to the Dubai Zoo. It's one of his earliest memories. He remembers nothing of the pilgrimage, not the Kaaba, the holy stone, not the millions of pilgrims: not even one. He remembers the car.

He doesn't remember Dubai, the cool, sleek floors of the hotel, the view, high rises under construction all round. These things all come from his mother, who remembers, vividly. He remembers not even the Zoo. White tigers. Birds of paradise. Chimpanzees, fighting, scrambling in the back, chasing one another in one great big, intergenerational feast of playing tag. All that comes from Aatifa.

Omar had noted none of it, nothing. He'd been at the wheel, of his first ever automobile. Red, racy. *His.*

It had been a push cart, one of the car-shaped ones for hire at the entrance of the Zoo. It was a hot day, a scorcher even for Dubai, the sun burning the lanes of the zoo to noxious, drooling strips of tar. His mother had watched, helpless, as Omar stood parked before the chimpanzees. She had been pointing out the mothers, the cute little baby monkeys, all to no avail. Omar refused to look up from the wheel. Aatifa had stood by, trapped in the sun, wrapped in her veils like a mummy, until, finally, she'd sought refuge in one of the bus shelter-like structures scattered about the Dubai Zoo: glass, air conditioned waiting rooms, not against any cold or wind, but against everything else.

His mother had spent the day in that refrigerated glass cube, watching her son crawl in and out of his automobile, under the sun, testing the plastic doors, the wheel, and refusing to budge--infatuated, for the first time, with the outside world, with a world outside her reach.

That night, on the bed, the cardigan had slipped from her shoulders, as Nouche had sat peering at the painting, the finger, with a glossy red nail, still in her mouth. She'd looked up at him through her lashes.

Before he knew it, he'd taken the plunge again, all over, and her tiny figure, so gracious and tense, had been dissolving under him, fanning out like something from a dream, something red and warm and wet, impossibly sleek and smooth, like an essence, an abstract of her, something all around.

She cried out, the red nails now grasping at the pillow, then waving in the air as she bit her own forearm.

He was plunging, he was lost in this red world, he was aiming for her, and no one else. This, too, was shocking, astounding. Unsettling. Unusual, to say the least. He gazed at her, afterwards. Her pale hands, those shiny nails.

She lay looking, again, at the canvas. It's nail enamel, she said at last.

What, Omar said.

Enamel, she repeated. For the shine.

She'd tried acrylics, she explained, then a coat or two of oils. Nothing worked. It was stuffy, she said. Earnest. Dull.

Omar nodded.

Early the next morning, Omar is standing alone, in his bathroom. He stares in the mirror. He needs to hurry. Seven minutes till dawn.
Time to eat. There's a blessing in sahur.

He looks down. Godzilla's still staring up.

Nouche, in bed the night before, had talked about the painting. It was static, she'd said. She'd been unable, somehow, to make it fly, to lift it from its meaning.

She'd waved in the air. To set it loose, she said, into abstraction.

He'd nodded. She'd scared him, just now, in bed. He did not want to talk. He dreaded what he might blurt out. Was he in *love*?
He wanted her to shut up, he wanted, most of all, to keep his own mouth shut, to be silent, and quiet. At peace.

Tonight, before the mirror, he is, however, still freaked out. He lusts after his own woman. With a passion.

He glances at his watch. He has five minutes to eat.

That evening, Nouche had brought her pale hand, her blood-red nails, to her mouth and yawned. Then glanced back at the canvas.

He'd sat gazing at that hand, still resting under her chin, and realised she had finished her work with this exact Chanel enamel.

The square at the centre had been set afloat. It hovered at the end of the tunnel, which itself was dislocated somehow from its setting. Dislodged.

It was a glistening passage, going no place, out of nowhere: disembodied flesh, brutal, vacant space. It was an essence, an abstract, of *her*.

Allah, Omar moans, gazing down, where Godzilla, with a final twitch of the head, lies deflating at last, in his hand.. It's a painting, he's thinking. I just got off on a *painting*. He stares in the mirror, shuddering still. Of *her*.
Omar peers in the glass, chilled, appalled and effusive, overflowing with happy confusion, a stupid grin on his face.

He glances at his watch. This took all of two minutes.
He looks out the window, which is dark, dead of night still, as far as Omar is concerned, but fuck me, he thinks. Verily. What does he know?

Back to the watch. Three minutes left. Three minutes left for sahur.

He is starved.

4

tuberose

She is in the bath.

The walls are black, the water a crystal looking glass, framed in the white enamel tub. In the watery mirror: her legs. Pale and shapely. She's shaving.

One red nailed hand is sliding down the razor, the other follows. It's a habit, checking for missed hairs, but really, in an absent-minded sort of way, Nouche is reaffirming those shins. Checking she's still here.

In the other room, the new painting is still leaning at the wall. A dark square, adrift in a sea of nail enamel red. It is finished, ready to be taken to the Shoreditch Gallery. She's worked on it all week. It now flies. It's a glistening abstract: a blood red vortex. *La Vide*.
The Void.

Nouche is in the bath now, soaking off paint and turpentine. Like an infusion, they're in her hair, in her skin, her pores. She floats in the tub, steeped in essential oils: bergamot and tuberose. They're expensive, these oils, and in direct defiance of the global recession, she's sprinkled them in liberally. She closes her eyes. Hair snakes out around her in the pale, lapping mirror. Her ears are submerged. They, too, are shut against the world. She drifts in silence, in tuberose, in the dark.

Nouche has a Brazilian waxist, a young mother, still fat from delivery, working out of a Shoreditch council estate, just around the corner from her gallery. It's a poky little flat, the waxing room carpeted in a faded pattern of purple and dust, a crusted cauldron in the corner.

How did she, Nouche wonders, drifting in her crystal sea, end up in a gallery in Shoreditch? She's Parisian. She was destined for the *Salon*.

Actually, Nouche's version of events is not entirely accurate. Nouche did not grow up in Paris. She's from Lille. Or, to be more exact, from *around* Lille. Even there, she's embellishing. Nouche is from Marly-Gomont, population

429, an hour south of Lille. An hour spent, as a teenager, every weekend, up and down, winding through Picardy, riding shotgun in some peasant boy's Renault. Marly-Gomont is a chocolate box hamlet sitting, she thinks, in a giant, green crater, an infinite saucer of nothingness. The only sound, on a summer's day, is the toll of the church bell, once, on the hour, resounding in the empty plate, and dying away, only to be revived, at last, fifty-nine minutes later.

She'd hated that church. She'd hated that bell. She'd hated Sundays, when, late and long after the party, like the village women, it got animated, at last, and vicious: clamouring, clubbing her over the head, the very essence of her migraine, her hangover--her skull throbbing with every godly, hateful toll.

She hated the women. She hated the single little street, soundless, as they'd ride in, those early Sunday mornings. Hated the quiet as she'd emerge from the car. As, eight hours later, she'd step from her mother's door for a pack of smokes. Hated the silence in the one cafe, where they stared at her, those women, their men, mute, until she slammed the door back shut behind her. Yes, she thought, she had managed to fuck the village's single black teen, a beefy kid with nappy hair, eldest son of the hamlet's one, utterly lost, Congolese family. That's how she learned posture. Not just gyrating in the front seat, to fit both their limbs between the gears and the doors and the dashboard, but right there in the cafe, those Sunday afternoons, little Minouche, clicking in and out in her heels to buy a pack of Gaulloise Blondes. Posture. From the door to the bar and back, parting like Moses the sea of dumb-struck villagers--her shoulders back, chin up, lip curled.

The kid had gone on to become a rapper, later, long after she'd moved to Lille, and then, to Paris, where she'd been, simply, Nouche. A famous rapper, actually, she smiles to herself, thinking of his nappy-haired head pulling faces in the *Marly-Gomont* video. It was edited in some friend's Lille flat a few years ago, that video, uploaded on YouTube, and promptly went viral, ending up a phenomenon: French, 'rural' rap, written up in Time magazine.

Fame. She, herself, had sort of been there. Almost. Half-way, pitched somewhere between the infamy of her teens and the career she'd imagined for herself in her thirties. Here she is though, approaching the end of that decade.

Here, in the Brick Lane bathroom. Her work not, as she'd envisioned, at the Pompidou, or Tate Modern. But around the corner from the waxist, on a wall in Shoreditch.

Her work has become strangely dormant, buried somehow, as though she herself is trapped in some long, dark, winter sleep. She is now, officially, more famous for who she's slept *with*.

Nouche lathers a handful of conditioner into her hair. She looks pale, not her own china tone but the flat white of her Dead Sea facial. Her eyes are dark, giant pools. She looks at her hands. The blood enamel of the painting, on her nails, the bare ring finger. A narrow band of that same Dead Sea white. The white band, where the ring used to sit, is an absence, a redux. It's pretty much all, she thinks, that's left of her fame. A negative.

She married Alain Mouille when she was twenty-three. *The* Mouille, the big, hairy host of *Soiree*, the France4 TV show.

Nouche sinks back again in the water, careful, this time, to not submerge the creamy hive on her head. She stares up at the ceiling. She'd met Mouille at twenty-two, still in art school, when he'd been a psychoanalyst with a degree in art theory and a small, exclusive practice. She had been impressed, like the other girls, at his lectures, unravelling the inner lives of Gauguin, of Godard, of the grand names of the public realm. Unlike the other girls, though, she'd had the fortune of possessing both posture and an air of ruin, clicking in and out of the auditorium in her heels, shoulders straight, hint of a smile, nose up in the air.

She'd grown up in a haystack. She'd grown up *poor*. She'd had nothing to begin with, not even her own body, which she'd lost, in that haystack, before she could remember, to someone who possessed her like cattle, someone who considered her his own.

She closes her eyes in the Dead Sea mask. This is one thought she is not about to chase to its conclusion, to its source, its origin. *Her* origin. Her genes, her blood. Blood sin. *No*. This is where this particular tunnel ends. Full stop.

A blood tunnel, she thinks, nonetheless. Blood red.

Alain had been on to her, on to her scent, the hint of sin she carried with such insouciance, a second-hand cashmere sweater draped around the blades of her shoulders. He'd followed her into the hallway, and out the building, into the street, down the steps of the Metro. There, as she'd been waiting on the platform, he stepped out, and, without thinking, shrugged off an extra large Pierre Cardin jacket, and knelt down, to spread it on the tiles before her. There it lay, on the platform, a maroon mix of silk and wool, with a light sheen, shining up at her. It made no sense, it was foolish, it was crazy, but it was the sincerest thing he'd done in a long time, and even if he stood there knowing he didn't know what it *meant*, staring at his jacket, he knew that he knew that he meant it.

It may, in all its absurdity, have been the one offering that Nouche could not have resisted. She'd sailed out into the world somehow, on that jacket, on that gesture. Out into the next fourteen years: into marriage and couture and the whole *Soiree* set: lights, parties at the Pompidou.

She'd watch from the director's suite, as the camera would cut from red-lipped starlet to politician, and back to Alain. From painter to film director, novelist back to starlet, and back, always, to the centre of the table, to Mouille. The table represented the nation, *L'Île de France*, City of Lights; Mouille at the heart, like a spider in a web, tying the acutely public, the entire domain of the *happening,* to the hidden selves of each of his guests, the world of the motive, of the private, the deep and static fount of desire, of heart and soul.

Nouche herself had been a bit of an icon, clicking around the studio. *La Petite Mouille*. She had sold most of her work before graduation. She'd hung from the immaculate white of whichever wall happened to be happening, her name, *La Mouille*, at one point making the careers of her dealers as much as they'd make hers.

Nouche now, half a decade later, opens her eyes, her face rigid in the mask. She soaks in the tub, the oils, steeps in cream, ridding herself of her paints. The new painting is finished, she thinks, over, ready, done. It seeps from her pores: the hard work, the coat after coat of oil, the constant worrying. The last lash of Chanel. *Done*.

Ready, she thinks, with a note of despair.

Alain had been the *Maitre d'* of Motive. Diviner of Drive. He had hit on her scent, teased out her wounds. The deeper she buried them under her elegance, her nonchalant click-click across the studio floor, the deeper he'd dug.

He'd come up for air, panting, as she lay on their left bank bed, her chin up, the smile still on her lips, but feeling turned inside-out, outside-in. She was caught in his web, where her public self had been tied, inexorably, to her innermost self.

He'd been Diviner of Desire, Master of ceremony, Host of the *Salon*. The spider pulling strings on *Soiree*. When he stopped loving her, the house came crashing down. Of course he'd slept with the red-lipped starlet.

She refuses to go into detail, Nouche, lying framed here by her East End bathroom walls. She refuses to go into the erroneous text message she received one Sunday morning, sent from his car. *Je suis sur la Periphe*, it read, I'm on the Motorway. She refuses to go into it, and she refuses to get out, out of its dull, *shallow* stupidity. *Miss you..* he'd continued *..et ta bouche profonde*. Your deep throat, she thinks, your deep dark mouth.

He'd no longer loved her. It wasn't her lips he missed, her deep dark mouth. Hers had not been anywhere near him, not that day, or the day before, or the days or weeks before that.

Hours later, or was it days--weeks, she really wouldn't know--she'd stood out on the Boulevard, gazing back at the massive double doors of their apartment. *Maison Mouille*. After fourteen years of marriage, this is where she'd found herself--divined, hosted, maitre-d'ed, her deepest, darkest self turned inside-out.

Then this. The flat, callous error. And here she was, at last: just turned out.

It's not unreasonable, she thinks, in the London bath, frozen in her mask. *C'est la vie*. Life, she thinks, death, whatever you want to call it. Hell.
Her hair sits in its cream hive. From the bathroom door, a silk dress hangs. Sheer white panties dangle from the towel rack. She glances down her body. It is, in fact, time for the waxist.

She thinks of the purple carpet. The Brazilian is struggling, with the baby, with the fat, and probably, she shudders, with the rent.

She thinks of the Shoreditch street, her gallery, the new painting. Finished, over, a thing of the past already.

Ready, she thinks.

What for?

Her eyes, black, giant pools, close in the Dead Sea face. The painting, newly finished, is stillborn, buried already in the silence around her, the winter sleep stretching out from her like the nothingness of Marly-Gomont.

It is a crater, this silence. It starts right here. In the crystal mirror of the bathtub, the black walls around her. It spreads from her pale limbs, adrift in water, adrift in tuberose. Spreads from her body, her heart, and out: to *L'Île de France*, to the Lights, to the *happening*.

Out, and out, it spreads: a tunnel of blood, and silence. Out. A deep dark throat, swallowing everything; cameras, lights. *Money*, she despairs. Fame. *Out*. It is an inner silence, her most private self, turned inside out, in full view, and stretching, stretching outward, to the very bounds of the nation, of the communal, of the public domain.

5

cry

Omar, in the Whitechapel Day Centre meeting, that Friday morning, wants to rip Billie Jean's heart out.

'I am more,' she has just concluded, 'Than the child of two addicts.'

When Omar came in nine months earlier, they took his money, his keys and his phone, stripped him, and took all his clothes, which had then been burned, or shredded, or chemically dissolved, he is unsure which: destroyed, in any case. Obliterated.

Now he sits in the meeting, feeling somehow naked, all over, again. It's Terry's turn to talk. To give feedback, not on anything Omar has said, but on the story just told by Billie Jean. She, today, is a newly successful artist, slathering women onto her canvases with a painter's knife: paintings which read *SHE CLAIMS I AM THE ONE*. She is here to chair the meeting. To give back what she received when *she* came in, now more than four years ago.

'I relate..' Terry says. 'To what you said about..' He is, in fact, struggling to relate, at all.

Anwar, too, sits looking at Billie Jean with a baffled smile. In black Converse high tops and jeans, her straight, skinny frame is more boyish than most of the men's around the table. Anwar leans back in his chair; his breasts, like two small puddings, resting on the soft bun of his belly. In the past nine months, he has not spoken once.

'..Proper wasted..?,' Terry tries.

Billie Jean, today, is far from wasted. She is all there. She exudes a raw glamor, an endurance of the present, of *pain,* that puts most of these men to shame.

She confuses Omar. He doesn't want her. He wants, he feels, with growing dread, to *be* her. This is such an unwelcome thought, he wants to flee the room. He sits staring at the door. Today he's a free man, a man surrendered. To God.

What does that mean, Omar thinks, if he now wants to be a *woman*?

Billie Jean is nodding at Anwar.

He has opened his mouth, as if to speak, but sits gazing at one of his nails, instead.

Billie Jean keeps looking at Anwar, until he looks up.

'I am more..' he says.

Billie Jean's straight shoulders nod in sympathy. Anwar sinks back in his chair, until, again, Billie Jean stares him out.

'Than the child..' Anwar says. 'Of..'

He returns to his nails.

Omar and Marquis shift uncomfortably in their seats. Terry opens his mouth. One glance from Billie Jean freezes all three of them.

Anwar speaks. '..Warring parents.'

Omar checks himself. It's true. He feels no desire, whatever, for this woman. None. He feels envy. Rage. An acute need to establish the packing order. He is sinking, feels lost, and helpless; impotent. Women, he thinks simply, *should not be this way.*

At home, later that afternoon. Dusk. The council flat. The land line. 'Yes,' he is nodding into the phone. 'I am fasting. I am praying, Mama.'

She gathers up again, as if rounding up the day, the circle of her children, his mother, calling each living child by name, touching lightly on professions, and family status, updating him, as is her habit, of the minutest change in each of her children's affairs.

He nods and listens as she talks, without menace, as she practices her particular brand of human interest, an interest in *blood,* wholly devoid of any of its usual connotations. *Blood* as Rumi, the Sufi Master, had put it,

A living, luminous flow.

She is luminous, his mother, beautiful. Even now. He pictures her by the door of her kitchen at dusk, framed by flowers hanging from the grilled fence of her ground floor flat. She was a beauty as a girl. He knows this not from photos, but from her stories, infers it from the backdrops to his childhood tales; the places in her mind's eye, the hanging gardens, the crystal transit lounges, the concourses.

Her tales are filled with fabled woodwork. Gilded walkways. Cool spots under domes made of lime and mud, and ancient beams. Light falling in at a slant.

She married his father, a rising star in Ethiopian diplomacy, shuttling between Addis and Asmara, when she was thirteen. Thirty-nine years ago. Left behind, after a homeland coup, the leafy North London residence he grew up in, and settled here, in a sprawling Tower Hamlets flat.

Thirty-nine years. He's not managed to stay paired with a woman for even one, Omar thinks. Or has he? He really couldn't remember. Like one of those early computer-animated videos--*Godley and Creme,* he thinks, *Cry*--his memory has been replaced by a succession of morphing features. The soft, pretty faces of his girls have all blurred together. He recalls more clearly the hardened jaws of other people's girlfriends. Those of his mates. The women Omar would invariably end up sleeping with.

Even then, more than their faces, Omar remembers the places they'd mated, the crack house rooms. He remembers a tree built from used needles, rising up from the floor, like a gleaming, skeleton Christmas tree.

His mother is saying, *Abebech.* He notes the tone of his sister's name on her tongue, his youngest sister, catches the high notes, their flow, their sweetness, rolling from his mother's lips.

The skeleton tree stands in his mind's eye, against the luminous flow of his mother's tale, a black tree, blood frozen in its needles.

He sits on the floor of his kitchen, holding on to the phone, amid the crack house walls of his own memories, of his own tales, as the spiked blood branches reach for the ceiling. He wonders what this backdrop might tell his mother about *him*; the tree of Death of his own fables, what *she* might infer from *that*.

'..*Baby*,' his mother is saying, meanwhile.

She sighs.

She said *baby*, and not to him--she wasn't talking *about* him, Omar suddenly realises.

He finds himself smiling, mutely, into the phone, a tear now rolling down his cheek. Before blurting out,

'I *know*.'

The baby. *Abebech*.

'I *know*,' he repeats, dumbly. His sister's *pregnant*.

The grin still sits on his face, wide as a boat, the smile itself now opening the gateways, it seems, of tears, of kin, of blood; a luminous flow coursing Omar's veins, lighting up his body, from the inside, as he sails away, on conversation, with his mother, into the sunset of her garden, the flowers hanging from the bars of her Tower Hamlets fence.

Dusk. Time for Omar to open the holy fast of Ramadan: a hasty swill of tea, too hot, glass after glass of water, standing by his kitchen tap, luke warm, but Omar has no patience to wait for the reserve of cool, life-giving liquid--which must exist somewhere underneath all this, the flat, the building, the estate--to find its way up the East London plumbing.

It is properly after evening prayers now. Time for *Iftar*: a handful of his girlfriend's rocket lettuce-- *organic*, he reads on the package--two cold samosas, half a left over ploughman's sandwich, all eaten straight from the fridge. Whatever.

Allah. He could eat a whale--a boar, a dog, for all he cares.

This is the problem with fasting. By the time he should eat he is beyond the edge of reason. *I know, I know,* he thinks, I should plan. Spend the daytime thinking about food, what to eat, where, when the day finally comes to a close and the blessed evening opens up before me.

He should, Omar thinks, spend the day like any good muslim, savouring every projected bite, shopping and cooking and preparing the table. But I have, Omar despairs, zero impulse control. If I think about food at all, it's usually because I look down and find I am half way through the packet of biscuits, already.

As it is, he just stands in the kitchen, in the half-dark, chewing another handful of rocket. His appetites are haywire these days, his belly as violently erratic as Godzilla below, a raging, unholy duet, a Godley and Creme of his own--of confusion.

You don't know how to ease my pain, his base instincts bellow from below. *You Make Me Wanna Cry*.

For all the haze of his former girlfriends, their faces blurred to one, generic smile, his current one, Nouche, seems carved into his retina. Every one of her lashes, every toe, each bloody nail is grafted into his cornea. Her terse body seems engraved in his mind's eye, as if slathered out of his own brain with one of Billy Jean's paint knifes.

This body, moreover, appears hardwired to the ungodly duo below, screaming *You don't know;* every stirring in his lower regions morphing into her face.

Omar stands in the cold glow of the fridge, eating hand after hand of dry lettuce. *Allah.* Just thinking of his hunger gives him a hard on. He can picture the dog, the boar, crying up from his groin, lip-synching the entire goddamn Godley and Creme video. *You don't know what the sound is darling, It's the sound of my teardrops falling.*

He is, in fact, a vegetarian. Loosely: it's in his blood, the house and the land he grew up in.

The pig meanwhile has, like everything else these days, shifted shape again, and taken on the face of his girlfriend, taking up the tune where the boar left off. *And you cheat,* she is miming, *And you lie,* and it's her lashes he sees, as he stands there chewing lettuce: her pearly toes, her sleek, waxy vulva, singing *CRY.*

There is no way to ease his pain, no way to soothe his urge, alone, in the kitchen, in the dark. He is caught in the light of the fridge, unable, suddenly, to go backwards or forwards, unable to breathe, for fear of losing it, altogether: losing this, his kitchen, his home, the nine months. His rebirth. Unable to breathe for fear of his screaming, raging urge to plunge--into her, or someone else, anyone, anything. The urge to plunge in a knife or an outfit. *You don't know how to play the game,* he thinks, crying.

You don't even know how to say goodbye. He is paralysed. Could he be losing her?

Is she slipping--or is she just dwarfed by his desire?

He panics at the grandiosity, the impossibility of his longing. At the urge to kill the need with the needle.
To creep back under the tree of Death, to spend his days among projectile stains, lame and wanking without hope or desire.

The boar is sneering. *You don't know what the sound is darling..*

The sound, he thinks, of outfits snapping, of needles crackling, as some junkie crosses the floor behind him. The sound of his own wrist, pumping nothing but dry blood, crusting on his foreskin.

Cry, he thinks, in the dark, in the kitchen. *Cry.*

The rest of the evening is improbable. It ends later, much later, well after midnight. But it starts here, just after dusk.
It starts with the bell. This is, of course, Nouche.

Not only is she dark and morose, she is terse, her very essence: like a coil or a spring, looped in and locked up, inside herself, inside her silence; waiting to be sprung. She is carrying a grocery bag from Sainsbury's, and a painting, wrapped up in plastic, which is dripping with rain. She is drunk.

Before he does anything else, that long, long Friday night, Omar is fed. This is not for the weak-hearted. Nouche, to put it mildly, is no vegetarian.

Raw meat, is what she rolls between her fingers, plucking bits of steak tartare straight from the bag, as she sits on the tiles of the kitchen, in the dark. Like his mother's, her interest in blood is without malice. She is here to feed him. Whatever else she may do tonight, before the moon strikes midnight, however she may choose to draw the curtain on this day, she has dropped her painting, the tunnel, the blood red passage, against the kitchen counter, and left it there, pooling on the kitchen floor. If it is an exit, it is one into the past, left behind, for now. She is here to feed Omar, and blood, raw, chopped, straight from the tray, is what she pushes, gently, with each bite, between his lips.

6

lover

By the time his girlfriend finally draws the curtain, that Friday, it is midnight. She is pictured against the powder blue drapes, cut off by the window frame like a Degas dancer. Like Degas' *petites danseuses*, she's straight and pale. There's something terse though, and inward, about her poise, her pose, something self-absorbed. Like a Michael Jackson moonwalk.
Across her shoulder-blades, a plummy cardigan. She turns around, and shrugs it off.

A YouTube playlist is dying away between her walls. It doesn't matter: Nouche, the dancer, is moving to a tune of her own. The cardigan hangs from one hand, from one shoulder, Michael Jackson style. *Billie Jean*, she's humming, *Is not my lover*.

Omar, meanwhile, is watching every move. Like her, he is caught in his own train of thought, hearing his own song. Omar is playing his own greatest hits, all of which, these days, revolve around *her*.

He is rewinding his favourite scenes, the parts--*her* parts: her body, his favourite bits--scratched onto his brain with a painter's knife. Omar has tunnel vision. Everything he looks at, these days, will turn into Nouche, eventually.

Now, by the end of this Friday night, he can see the red brassiere against her pale shoulders. He could count her lashes. He could reach out and lift her, between her legs, lift her from her pearly toes onto the bed.
It is late.

This is how this particular day, Friday, in the holy month of Ramadan, will end. All this, the moonwalk, the curtain, Omar's vision occurs around midnight.

Now: how it started. Friday began, for Omar, with the meeting at the Whitechapel Day Centre, where, nine months earlier, for the first time in seventeen years, he got clean.

A meeting chaired by Billie Jean, as it happened, who, four years into the programme, carried her brave, bruised heart on her sleeve. She was tiny, in high-tops and skinny jeans, wearing her raw, lion's heart inside-out, on her skin, like a coat of armour. That morning, she had shrugged her boyish shoulders in sympathy, as Omar's peers, grown men, had sat in the meeting, and cried.

By the time the first tears flowed in the Day Centre, Nouche, on Brick Lane, had just been getting out of bed. She was taking the new painting to the Shoreditch Gallery, around the corner--Nouche thought, stepping into her panties--from her waxist, the Brazilian, the young mother working out of her council flat. Nouche needs a different waxist. She'd pictured the flat, carpeted in dusty polypropylene, bills stacking up among the purple tufts. Nouche wanted marble floors.

The canvas, that Friday morning, was impractically large. It was wrapped up in layers of plastic. Even descending her own stairs in a cloak and heels, she had trouble not tumbling down after it. Walking down to Spitalfield market for a cab, passing Gilbert and George's listed Fournier Street facade, she worried about the wind catching her work like a sail, and carrying her off with it, out into the stratosphere, not the one of Georgian townhouses and openings and cocktails at Tate Modern, *cameras*, she thinks, *lights*--but the silent *nowhere*, beyond, of stumbling down the street alone in the wind: the outer space of Marly-Gomont, of the haystack she grew up in. The nowhere of divorce, of her TV-host ex-husband's *Soiree* set gone dark, the stars all blacked out.

She flags down the cab. The driver--an obese man with the kind of inbred, pit-bull look she would, in any other scenario, have been scrambling away from--just sits there, and so she finds herself, this Friday morning, in the reverse kind of scene where she is knocking herself about, trying to cram both her body and the painting *into* the serial killer's car.

Then it's time to repeat the whole thing, backwards, and she ends up ten pounds poorer, on the Shoreditch pavement, with the painting, in the wind, which is now a wet, drizzly kind of daytime darkness blowing up her skirt and down her cloak, her cleavage; a persistent, cold sneeze in her neck. The shop is closed.

The Shoreditch Gallery. It's dark. She checks her phone, for the date, the time. Did she not talk to her dealer this morning? Did he not tell her to drop in any time? She redials the number. It is now starting to, seriously, rain.

Paul.. she starts.

Nouche, he booms on the other end. *Cherie*.

Where are you pumpkin, she says.

Au Salon, he croons. His broken French is moderated by a low bass, the kind of deep, broad-chested voice she associates with Mouille, the ex-husband; with large men in Cardin, with Gaulloise. It makes her sleepy. Makes her want to sit down on the pavement and close her eyes and listen, as if she's on the line with Barry White. Paul could be telling her he's about to burn all her hair off; all she will hear, right now, is *Don't Go Changing*.

I Love You Just the Way You Are, Paul is singing. Hang on, she thinks.

Anytime, my darling, she hears now, actually spoken, by Paul, into the phone. Still in Barry White's voice. *Drop in anytime*, he is saying. *Cherie.*

Part of her wants to murmur back into the phone, *I will darling*--wants to go to sleep on his chest. Part of her wants to scream.

'I'm here..' she says, peering into the dark window, in the rain. There is something overly bright about the gloom inside.

'Righto,' Paul interrupts her, in a brisk Cockney pitch now. 'Hold on a sec, luv.'
There is a crack somewhere in the background, then silence.

She waits, until the line goes dead, then drops the phone. She is still gazing in the dark tunnel of the gallery window. That blankness. The long wall. It's empty.

She redials. The line, of course, is silent. She listens as the phone rings, in the wind and the rain, until, finally, somewhere on the other side, inside the Shoreditch Gallery, somewhere down that long, bare wall, Paul's voicemail clicks on, booming, once more, in the Barry White voice. *Hey..*

Minutes, or hours, later, she, the painting, and her soaked little cloak are draped around the bar. A musician, a kid with a violin she keeps taking for a skate board, is gesturing for a refill. Still later, she is lying spread eagled around the corner, on a table, the Brazilian, the waxist, the one with the baby, working away, with both hands, at her crotch. The Brazilian rips at the wax as if Nouche, between her legs, has grown a bear. She holds up each furry strip in triumph, like a headhunter, as if she's scalping some private animal kingdom.

Nouche, at this point, is beyond caring. She drank away the afternoon with the kid with the skate board. Violin, she corrects herself. The kid with the violin. Though the instrument had been covered in graffiti, it had sounded nothing like a skate board. He'd played her *Billie Jean*.

Now, the rain has stopped, and a weak light plays with the dust of the purple carpet. Nouche lies, her toes pointing to opposite ends of the table, her vulva rising in the middle, like a silver moon. She lies on the waxist's table and--as she will when moonwalking later, that midnight--hums.

Omar, around this time, is on the phone himself, on the landline. He is rounding up another day in the holy month of Ramadan--talking and sailing away into the sunset with his mother.

Later this Friday, later tonight, he will kneel before an empty fridge, and cry. Still later he will lick raw blood from his girlfriend's fingers, and hold her, rocking, on the kitchen floor.

Now, though, it is late afternoon, and she is back on the street, lugging, still, her painting, and squinting in the light. Shoreditch is still windswept, and Nouche is now both more sluggish, and more light-headed, than this morning. She pauses in front of another window, another gallery, one reading *She Says*.

Nouche picks up the painting, and clicks on, in her heels. A gust of wind catches her cloak. She ducks into the doorway to pull down the maroon hem, then steps out again, before the gallery's second window, which says,

I Am The One.

It's a different show from one she saw lat month, in the eighth floor flat. Same stuff, though: De Kooning-style nudes, with a touch of Francis Bacon in the middle, splotches of red. Billie Jean.

Again the wind threatens to take hold of her own canvas, again she has visions of being lifted, like Dorothy, in her heels, and skirted off into the sky, not to Oz, but instead--in another one of today's movie reversals, like cinematic moonwalks--to be whirled straight back to her own private Kansas, Marly-Gomont.

Marly-Gomont. Poison green, like Van Gogh's peasant cafe, like a green moonscape, a crater, around the haystack where she was deflowered, in silence; the only sound the single, hourly, toll of the bell.

By the time the waxist had finished, just now, Nouche's buzz had been wearing off. The kid, the violin, the Cabernet had drained from her system, and she'd been breaking for the waxist's doorway, away from the stench of lactation, of reused shopping bags and unpaid bills, pulling her wallet and practically throwing cash at the Brazilian. Her twenty pound notes had still floated there, over the purple polypropylene pile of the carpet, while Nouche herself had already been outside the building, possessing neither the patience to wait for

50

her change, nor the desire to touch anything, ever again, in or from that council estate.

Nouche is now standing in the street, pretty much broke, holding on to her painting in the sun, in the wind, in the glow, from the gallery's window. The glow of Billie Jean's rising star. She waits to be Oz-zed off to Kansas, to the silent meals of her youth, the bare kitchen table, the ice box empty save a stinking pint from a home-milked cow.

She hates, with a vengeance, Alain Mouille, she hates the show, *Soiree*. She hates this other show, Billie Jean's, in the stupid window. *She Says I'm The One*. She hates, she thinks, even Michael Jackson, hates the stars: all of them, their rich-and-famous faces. She hates the sun, and the wind, as she stands here on the Shoreditch pavement, about to be tunnelled off, herself, into extinction, into poverty, into nowhere: the Van Gogh landscape of her childhood, Marly-Gomont, the crater, like a black moonscape, *Starry Night*--the lights all painted out.

It is time, she decides, for another drink.

Omar, by then, hangs up the phone. He is smiling, still, the same smile he was wearing just now, wide as a boat, on the line with his mother. His sister, Abebech, is having a *baby*.

It is an hour or so later, that this particular buzz, too, has burned off, and he stands in front of the fridge, chewing on cold, dry rocket lettuce. Organic. Hers.

This is when Omar is having his own flashes of Billie Jean's painter's knife: in the visions of Nouche, carved into his skull. The same ones he will be having at midnight. Now, though, it's dusk. Iftar, time to open the holy fast. The fridge is barren, save his girlfriend's greens. He could eat a pig.

He has a hard-on just thinking. This is where his hunger goes haywire: where the unholy trinity of his desire, for sex, drugs and food, has created a direct pathway, a neuro-superhighway, from his groin to straight to his brain. And on. A tunnel, right into her body.

It's splayed before him, like a pig's carcass, Francis Bacon style.

Later, she stumbles into the flat, with a wrapped up, dripping painting, and a Sainsbury's carrier bag. Still later that night, she moonwalks in front of the powder blue curtain, undressing before Omar's eyes. But that is not now. Now, she is hungry. She drops the painting, sinks down beside him on the floor, in the dark, and feeds him raw meat, with her fingers, straight from the bag, straight from the container. Pushes bite after bite into their mouths.

Then she nods, and passes out.

He holds her, on the kitchen floor.

The intensity, the immensity of his desire, immobilises him, for the moment. He simply can not take this. It is too much. He holds her, gnashing his teeth. He cries.

It's the baby. He doesn't know this.

Omar is only nine months old, himself. Nine months, only, of feeling anything at all. His nerve ends, like Billie Jean's, glower on his skin, fester and ache. He is exposed, like a newborn, his skin just another organ.

It is open, his skin, permeable, unsecured. He feels defenceless, like one of those trinkets displayed on bits of velvet cardboard, as he wanders around Tower Hamlets sometimes, negotiating gangs and bike thieves, lock picks and jihad recruiters, burglars and plain old scum; and yet this is nothing compared to the way he feels here, tonight, in his own kitchen, in the arms of his own girlfriend, whose limbs are grafted to his baby ones, whose face is grafted onto his own, whose lashes and toes, whose deep dark passage, lead straight into his groin, his neural pathways, into his infant brain. There, his urges all connect: a single cry.

All he wants to do is sob.

He wants sugar, and milk--sweetness, honey, the nectar of her passage, of her insides, as she clasps her toes around him. He wants it mindlessly. He wants it only.
He reaches for her feet, and takes off her heels.

Then, on the kitchen floor, he cries.

Omar cries like a baby. He sobs into her hair.

He cries, for minutes, hours, a long time, perhaps just seconds, after all. Something shifts, something happens, and he finds that this is it, the thing inside him, the urge: it is the need for tears themselves, this flood streaming down his cheeks and chin, carrying with it the very things he's been clinging to for life.

It's his fear, that's streaming out. Fears he never even knew he carried, of being barren, of ending his line, of extinction. Fear of death. There it goes, out with the water, for the moment. Next is relief, the joy of his sister's conception. Still he cries, extracting from himself even this pleasure, in his tears, a living, luminous flow, streaming from him in great heaves until finally, he lies beside her, his woman, feeling empty, feeling drained, feeling calm and present, and sleepy, until at last he is no longer driven, but drifts himself, safe within her arms, out into the blissful sea of equanimity. Surrendered, he half thinks, half sleeps, half dreams: to the One Love of the Sufis, of his childhood. To God.

She wakes, moments later, with a head ache. She thinks, first, of the painting, and groans. It leans against the counter, wrapped in plastic, wettish, but, she thinks, apparently alright. What's she doing, though, beneath a counter, on Omar's kitchen floor? She groans again, thinking of the canvas, and her heels, and the long way home in the dark, windy night, back to the comfort of her black sheets, her bed. She needs down cushions, silk pillow cases. Now.

She needs *money*, she thinks.

This thought, at some level, catches her by surprise. She wonders if she's still drunk. She decides she is, probably, instead, not drunk enough, and gropes around, in the dark, for her shoes. It's the real beauty of Brick Lane, she thinks. It never sleeps. Unlike her gallery, she groans, again, which is now officially, she supposes, comatose. Which is probably beyond the sleep of the living, which is, in all likeliness, probably dead. Like her career, which, unlike Brick Lane, seems to never wake, which is, she muses darkly, worse than dead, her paintings dead on arrival, not to be resuscitated. Not even the Blood of Christ, she thinks, will revive her work, as she hates Him, hanging from the cross over the bare table of her childhood, banging that single note as she'd get banged in the haystack under the church clock, she hates him with a Passion normally reserved for the poor--or the rich, of course. The Stars. She is, she admits, perhaps a little pickled still.

Omar, around this time, too, finds himself waking, drifting back out of sleep, out of the deep sea of equanimity, of the living: the luminous flow, of Islam, of Surrender.

He watches her stretch, get up, watches her red-nailed fingers smooth down her skirt, the little cloak, watches her stockinged feet step into her heels.

'Leave it,' he says.

'Leave the painting here. I'll take it round,' he adds. 'In the morning.'

She nods, glancing at it, and lights a Gaulloise Blonde. She exhales. 'Thanks,' she says.

Bon soir.

Omar is alright after that. He is alright for the moment, as he crosses the lounge in the moonlight, on his way to his own bed, a strange, slow kind of moonwalk, still submerged in the ocean of life. The sea of the Sufi masters. Surrendered, to this life, to God.

He's alright, alone in his bed.

It is later, that the visions start. Nouche, by then, is drawing her curtain. She clicks her fingers, and hums.

It's a syncopated beat, a split beat, like the one of her heart. It is pounding, her heart, a split, blind rhythm, propelling her forward, into the night.

It's driving her on, one foot in front of the other--one heel in the past, one stockinged toe in the future. A split beat, moving her on, the floor lighting up under her soles, like blue squares, like the squares under Michael Jackson, singing *I Am The One*.

One foot in the past, one in the future. Pissing on the present, on god; pissed off, or just plain pissed. Whatever, she thinks. She is doing her moonwalk.

This is when Omar's buzz, the God thing, starts wearing off. He is in bed, alone.

He's back at square one.

She dances before him, her body Bacon-ed into his skull with a knife. No, she's not in the room. She is worse. She is poor and depressed, somewhere just outside his scope, outside his Vision. Is she suicidal? He doesn't know. She moves to her own tune, which is silent, a private moonwalk, performed in plain view but out of reach, out of touch, in some parallel realm of her own.

She moves before him, impervious to Rumi, the Sufi masters, to the Living, luminous flow. She is humming.

Omar is alone. It is midnight. His girlfriend is splayed before him, a pornographic version of her he doubts she would approve of, although it is certainly *her,* her essence, an abstract of her, even sharper, terser, than the actual spring of her own body.

It stares at him, this body, making him insane. He cannot remember with any accuracy the faces of even one of his girlfriends, before her. He is used to seeing with precision only the others, the ones he'd get at in the dark, behind some back or the other, the ones he'd turn to the wall, or the ones he would call up in private, from a life of violence, of women tormented and displayed on film, in magazines, online, for this particular purpose.

Today, he is tortured by his own woman. This makes him want to cry. All over. Is he a man?

He wonders, thinking of Billie Jean's stoic face at the Whitechapel Day Centre, this morning. He'd felt no desire for her, no want whatsoever, just rage, and envy: he'd wanted to be *like* her. He wanted her place in the scheme of things: her heart, her endurance in the face of pain.

You don't, he imagines her sneering, lip-synching the words to Godley and Creme.
You don't even know

How to play the game.

56

He'd wanted to rip it out, her heart, and eat it.

He himself, is helpless. He is possessed.
He needs his cock back, he thinks. Pronto. Now.

Then it dawns on him. Nouche is his, for the taking. He can do with her as he
bloody well likes. God, he thinks, will understand. God knows he's at the end
of his tether.

She dances, in his mind's eye, in her window, shrugging off her cardigan, and
humming *Billie Jean*.

Next, she is splayed on the table, and then on the floor, she is more bacon than
Francis Bacon. She is the deep, red passage of her painting, the pulpy mess of
his own brain carved in her image with the paint knife, like Adam fashioned
after Eve. She is the very putty of lust.

This is where it's her, he imagines miming the song--not Billie Jean. *And you
cheat, And you lie..*

Cry, she taunts.

Nouche herself, meanwhile, is singing a different tune altogether. YouTube
fades from her room. She hums, doing the moonwalk, in front of the curtain.

Then she is on her satin sheets, her toes pointing in different directions, the past
and the future, as she herself sinks away in the centre, escaping both, for the
moment, as she moonwalks somewhere in the middle, in silence, down--down
the passage marked, for the present, *WAY OUT*

Omar, helpless, needs to start over. *You Cheat,* Godzilla cries, cringing, from below. *You Lie*.

He needs truth. It is a hunger inside of him, it's the God thing, he supposes, a force greater even than the unholy trinity of his appetites combined, put together, a hunger deeper and more dementing even than his hunger for filth, for crack, for gear, for the body imprinted on his retina, a hunger perhaps underlying, fuelling even, in the greater scheme of things, all his other appetites, as they converge and spike, this night, in his desire for her, his own woman, the one scratched, with an old, used needle, onto his eyeballs.

Allah.

Here she is again, willing, pliant. He enters her again, feeling free this time, light headed suddenly, heady with his sense of purpose, divine purpose, he feels, as if he has succeeded, finally, in transmogrifying Billie Jean's courage, in eating, and incorporating, at last, her lion's heart. He is here to take possession, of his desires, of his woman, of himself. He is here to fuck. God knows he *wants* to.

This is where he is flooded, not just with the bliss of the moment, and, finally, ungrudgingly, his own seed--but with truth, with *pain*.
It's sweetness he's been craving, all along, the Mother of Desire, sugar and milk. Sweetness he's been hungry *for*. The pot of honey, at the end of the rainbow, at the end of the tunnel, the end of the passage. Sweetness: her deep dark throat, as *she* comes, contracting around *him*.

He is shattered, alone in his bed: his courage, his possession fractured, scattered, cast out, washed into the sea, the dead wide ocean of the night. He is lost, held together by no more than honey, the honey of her rainbow, of her contractions, her essence--held by nothing but the nectar, the sweet ambrosia of *her*.

He is beyond hope or reason, Omar despairs. The dumb, wide, grin is back on his face, as he cries in the dark.

He is in love.

She meanwhile, at just this moment, actually *is* coming, too, is orgasming, through some strange feat of synchronicity, herself. Her lover, like Omar, is heavy: hard and boyish. That is, Nouche decides, what she, in the end, must like most about her.

She is solid, raw and manned up, with an air of dominion, like the Lion King. Billie Jean, Nouche decides, is just *like* Omar.

Christ knows how these things work, she thinks, nodding off, or passing out. Blacking out, in any case. Exiting the stage. Billie Jean is now her lover, God only knows how or why, and Nouche has fallen asleep, sailed out on her own perplexity, and hoping, in some corner of her mind, the single bit of light still on in a sea of dark, that *He* will understand.

7

cat

Winter falls early in Aatifa's Tower Hamlets kitchen. The clock has fallen back, in the early Sunday hours, and it is now, suddenly, black as night. Nouche lights a Gaulloise Blonde at the kitchen table. Her flame lights up the walls, the Arab scrawl framed over the furnace, the portraits of Aatifa's children, Omar's siblings. Omar sits across from her, in the dark, his face briefly glowing in the flare.

Aatifa herself left the kitchen in the middle of preparations for dinner. This now seems hours earlier: when it was light still, and afternoon--which is, in fact, just minutes ago. Aatifa left to pick up the phone in the next room. They can hear her talking, through the kitchen door.

Aatifa's voice, from the sealed lounge, is both wildly exotic, and utterly familiar, depending on your point of observation. It's like Schrödinger's cat. In this quantum physicist's thought-experiment, a cat is locked in a sealed room, where the state of a particular subatomic particle determines whether it will live or die.
The catch is that the particle's condition, theoretically, is subjective, depending on whether or not we are looking. Until we open the door, the cat is thus famously, and absurdly, both alive and dead.
The cat may stand, tonight, for our glaring incapacity to grasp even the most basic facts of our own lives--let alone the world at large.

Back to Aatifa, still in the other room, still speaking on the phone. The couple here, sitting in the dark.

Nouche, the Parisian, in a pleated silk dress and heels, hears a high-pitched chatter she associates with markets, with auctions, with, for some reason, red and white: with the cream of silk garments; and scarlet--with raw slabs of meat.

Omar hears his mum. He hears the easy conversation, the luminous flow, of kin, of blood. He hears her talking to his sister, Aatifa's voice muted behind the door. His baby sister, Abebech, who got married at twenty-two this summer, and who will be three months pregnant this week.

Nouche's Gaulloise is a star between them in the dark. She would not have lit it in front of his mother, who neither smokes, or drinks, or wears, for that matter, the silk skirts and shiny, ultra-sheer stockings Nouche herself favours. Nouche, who is thirty-eight, divorced, and childless. Not to mention slightly drunk, which, fortunately, is not something Aatifa would notice, as she has so rarely in her fifty-two years encountered a real-life bottle, its effects would take some actual pointing out.

Neither Nouche, nor Omar, is in fact, really, listening to Aatifa. Here, dusk has fallen, an hour early, before dinner; night has descended over the kitchen counter, over a pale blue tea towel, over the open bowls and chopping boards strewn with peels and diced bits, a cleaver gleaming softly as Nouche, again, inhales.

Nouche is listening not to Aatifa but, instead, to Omar, whose lips glow in the dark. He, in turn, is miming words, phrases which, just minutes ago, lay out in the daylight between them, neatly lined in the open notebook on the table, and which now, like the terry towel, the food, the counter, the framed pictures, have disappeared into the wintertime night, so suddenly upon them. They float between them, now, those lines, as rumours only, tremors, on Omar's tongue.

He whispers, *That is how speech does*

Silk on one side
Cheap, striped canvas on the other

Omar is quoting Rumi, the Sufi master. He is quoting ancient Persian, muslim poetry.
He is, however, also talking about writing itself, drawing attention to the poems he himself has been writing, which is what the notebook, now near invisible on the table, contains. Drawing attention to the fact that these poems, silken as they may sound, were drafted, sketched out, fabricated. Voiced.

Nouche is listening to this as she smokes. She hears Omar's low notes emitted in the dark, spun between them, like silk. Inhaling, she sees both the sheen of speech, its finish, its glow--and, as she exhales, the Gaulloise going dim, she sees the matt canvas, the cheap linen, the drawing board, of Omar himself: his lips moving in the night, tongue and throat, to be guessed at only in the dark, the baritone of his chest, his heart. The other side of speech, the canvas, where this, his voice, is not yet art: it's craft.

Nouche knows about canvas. She is a painter. She knows about coat upon coat, layer after layer of oils. She knows a silk gloss varnish from cheap, coarse linen, knows the front of her canvas, from the back.

They have been working together. Nouche paints tunnels, passages, things marked *WAY OUT*.
Omar talks.
His voice is a tunnel of its own, channeling Rumi, the Sufis, his childhood faith.
The faith of his mother, still talking, in the other room.

Aatifa couldn't know that with the Parisian at her kitchen table, she has not so much gained a daughter, as recovered a son. Omar could no more have told his mother what crack has done to his life over the past seventeen years, than he could have spoken to her from the grave. His mother has less conception, even, of drugs than she has of drink. The crack-house floors Omar used to wake on, five inches deep in waste, in discarded syringes, in strangers, stretched out on beds of splintered needles, sometimes dead for days.

Today, clean less than a year, Omar sits at his mother's table at dusk: a large, black outline against the kitchen tiles. The holy month of Ramadan has come and gone. Eid has come, with its tide of magnanimity and forgiveness, but nothing could have bridged the sheer abyss between life as he has known it until eleven months ago, and this, his mother's kitchen--except for this single, miraculous fact: that he is sitting here *clean*.

This is one tunnel Omar has crossed, one passage he's traversed, one exit he's found.

Here he sits at the table, in the dark, with a beautiful woman, a woman from

France.

She paints, he whispers.

Nouche listens. Omar has moved on to a poem of his own.

She spells
WAY OUT

Eyes closed
Legs open

Like anything.., Omar continues, reciting from memory--the lines, the table, the kitchen, the notebook lost in the dark--.*.Like faith, like sin..*

WAY OUT
Is spelled
Backwards
Blind.

Blindly, he whispers. *Baby.*

WAY OUT
Is spelled
WAY IN

The poem's called *IN*. Unlike the painting it refers to, her painting, one she lugged all over the East End, one wet, windy day two months ago. The red tunnel, ending in a single square. Titled *OUT*.

In the kitchen, today, they are tying her exit to his entrance, his ins to her outs: putting Omar's words to her image: a collaboration of sorts. He has been invited to read at the Whitechapel Day Centre, the place where, not a year ago, they burned all his clothes. Now, his peers, the small group left of those he came in with--Terry, Marquis, Anwar--have offered to host an evening of drugs-free street culture, with him, Omar, headlining. Nouche's tunnel paintings will be part of Omar's spoken word performance, with the borough of Tower Hamlets funding a video recording, to go onto the council website, and, of course, on YouTube.

Cameras. Lights.

Listening to Omar in the dark, in the Tower Hamlets kitchen, Nouche is closer than she has been in eighteen months, to the Paris world she left behind. The world of *Soiree,* of Alain Mouille, her TV host ex-husband. The Paris of rock starlets, of champagne and books, of authors and conceptual artists gathered around Mouille's table, of politics and couture and desire discussed under the cascading crystal of studio armatures.

Aatifa, just now, bursts through the door, a tall, dark woman in white robes, long fingers catching the switch on the wall.

Both Omar and Nouche sit blinking in the sudden flood of light, the neon strip crackling overhead.

What, Aatifa hollers, Are you two children sitting here for, in the dark?

She picks up the cleaver, and slashes an onion. *Allah*, she says, looking up at the wintertime clock. 'It's come midnight,' she says, 'Before it's afternoon.'

It is Aatifa, that evening, who returns Nouche to the City of Lights. Aatifa, who was born not here, in Tower Hamlets, who, in fact, has relatively recently settled in the large, ground floor council flat. Aatifa has lived half her life in Hampstead, in the leafy North London diplomat's residency Omar grew up in.

To Aatifa, there has been no crackhead Omar. There is the baby she drove around with, in Asmara, in the back of a white Peugeot 504, the driver in front sweating as he swerved the main potholes on the broad boulevards leading to her young husband's offices.
There's the toddler asleep in her lap, in Addis or Khartoum or Djibouti, as a

porter would appear from some terminal with her family's luggage; the stack of cases topping his head, the porter's short, bow legs, all mirrored across a marble airport floor.

There's the Omar ignoring the Dubai Zoo apes as he spent a blistering noon getting in and and out of a signal red push car, getting behind the wheel of his first ever automobile.

There is, to Aatifa, the Omar reading under the trees in the Hampstead garden, the tall youth running in place in the driveway, weightlessly moving on the concrete, suspended among the roses, as she would watch from the kitchen window; the long-limbed youth almost levitated over her lawn, until, in one split moment, she would look up and he would be gone, her lawn deserted, dust visibly whirling the air.

There is the man, tonight, at the council kitchen table.

The years between, in ways fundamentally inexplicable, not least to Aatifa herself, have, like Schrödinger's poor cat, been both dead and alive; have both happened and not happened, depending on the point of observation.

Yes, of course, there has been the morning when, instead of reappearing around the Hampstead corner, pearly drops streaming into the soft terry cotton neck of his sweat suit, Omar remained the absence left on her lawn. The dust in the air, the empty imprint. There's been the morning when Omar was left suspended somehow in her driveway: something only *waiting* to happen. Does that mean it happened?

And yes, of course there have been years in between. There were light-years, between the North London home, and the Tower Hamlets estate. The homeland war, her husband's fall, may have been the least of it. There has been murder. There's been death matching that of Omar's absence.

Omar's absence. The shadow years, when he had dissected himself from Aatifa, removed himself at the root. The root, which was a craving. In his heart, where the two, the need for his mother, and for a stupor, were both the same thing, and mutually exclusive.

Neither of them, Omar or his mother, will talk of the Omar hiding under Aatifa's robes in the car, as the young driver would speed them through the dark, through the night, where blood ran black, potholes filling up with bumps it bore no thinking about, a night too bewildering to even start organising it in terms of kin or clan, coming or going, ins or outs.
When human ties, blood ties, become, just simply, *blood*..
When blood, instead of flowing, slow and luminous, starts simply pouring out into the street.. What does that mean in terms of Schrödinger's cat: *what,* then, is it, you're observing? What is it, even, that may or may not be happening?

Omar, like his mother, has things to remember and things to, more pressingly, forget.

To Omar, up till the age of twenty-one, the impulse to shut down may have been identical, to the one to hide in his mother's robes. Up till the age of twenty-one, he and his mother would forget together, side by side, her slicing onions in the kitchen, him running in place in the driveway.
Then one day--off he sprinted.

He must have run, at some point, into kids he didn't know, got offered things he'd not seen before. Beer, a spliff, the usual perhaps on most Hampstead lawns, excluding, of course, his own. In any case. Forgetting, once tried among peers, separate from his own clan, proved a habit there was no turning back from. It became a need of its own, and then an absence, a negation in its own right, the way out--the empty imprint left in Aatifa's life, a massive black-out in his own. Did *any* of that ever *happen*?

Here he is in the kitchen, watching Nouche stretch her sheer, slender legs and click across the kitchen floor. Her back, in cream silk, is tiny, beside his mother's great white robe at the counter. Nouche runs the tap, her half-smoked Gaulloise hissing out. Nouche's back is slight next to Aatifa's imposing taft, but just as straight; the women like negatives, somehow, of some same, basic principle.
Aatifa was built to traverse the marble floors of one or the other North African terminal. A child asleep on her hip, a porter teetering under her cases her robes

and gowns.

Nouche was made to be lit with perfection, crystal reflecting every small curve, every angle; to cross a Paris studio floor in her heels.

Watching both women, side by side at the Tower Hamlets council kitchen counter, Omar is not sure wether to get on his knees, and kiss the ground they stand on--or to cry.

Aatifa shakes the onions from the board, into a pot, and hands the knife to Nouche, who sticks it under the tap, and slips it onto the drying rack. Both may be naturals when it comes to wielding big, razor knifes, to cutting away at the past--both have the shoulders, the posture to proof it.

Nouche did not grow up in Paris. She is from Marly-Gomont, a Northern hamlet of scrawny, home milked cows lost in flat fields stretching all around. A place of inbred women gossiping under the church clock, its blunt little steeple Marly-Gomont's single aspiration, the one thing, lamely, reaching for the sky.

She married Mouille at twenty-three, still in art school. A large, gregarious man, with a lust for getting to the bottom, a man who turned her inside out. She hates him, still, with a vengeance, his penetrating mind, his endless probings, his showy, moneyed appetites, all leading nowhere, dead-ending in a shallow, sordid divorce.

She now lives in a single room in the East End, opposite the mosque. This is where she met Omar, a week clean. Eleven months ago. On the street, thrown out of the building, where he had gone to pray.

Crackhead Omar. The one who, like the cat, is, and isn't, here, today, in Aatifa's kitchen. Crackhead Omar had lived in the street, on whatever he could pilfer from the pavement, from the stones. He was banned from hospitals and hostels, had been barred from every shop or store in Tower Hamlets, was routinely thrown out at church fetes and charity bazars.

He'd been turned away, that morning, at the Brick Lane Mosque.

Nouche had just stepped from her door that same December morning, to unlock her bike. It had been her third in two months, chained to the grill fence across the street, right before the mosque's entrance, where, she hoped, the constant coming and going of slippered men, all through the night, would somehow safeguard it. Their murmurings, escaping from the soft-lit hallway, the stained glass windows, would, like a mantra, a spell, keep the bike safe, she'd pray, from the thieving Brick Lane night, each night, till dawn.

Omar had sat by the doors, that winter morning, on the ground, in a new white shirt and too-wide pants, as she clicked into the street. A dark face, like any other, perhaps a bit more anguished, more determined, more raw. There was something about him, she'd found herself thinking, halfway across the road, for no reason at all in the world. Just that. *There is something about him.*

The bike was gone.

What Aatifa doesn't know is that, instead of gaining a daughter, with Nouche, she has recovered her son. To Aatifa, there is no Crackhead Omar. There is no crack. There is little Omar, and there's the man she knows, without having to check, to be sitting behind her, at the table, as she stirs the pot.

Of course, there have been light-years, between the North London driveway, her fitted Hampstead kitchen--and this, the cramped counter, the chipped council furnace. There has been murder. There's been another war, and another. There's been blood. She has lost uncles, cousins.
Nayla.

There has been death, matching that of Omar's absence, of whatever was left of his life--the Tree of Death, built from broken needles, like a skeleton Christmas tree. The tree he'd hulked under, on a crack house floor; the people sleeping beside him, to never wake again.

Aatifa lost a child.

There's been death, matching Omar's--bone by bone.

Has any of it happened? She empties a bowl of mushrooms in the pot. The *ijeras* are done, her *wat* is bubbling away. Aatifa hands the bowl and the cutting board to Nouche, who leaves them dripping beside the cleaver in the rack. Behind them, Omar's chair scrapes on the lino. He appears beside the women at the counter, his tall, broad back next to Nouche's silk pleats, and his mothers gown, his large hands holding nothing, not a clue, to any of it. Wielding nothing but a kitchen towel; his mother's dish cloth.

Nouche had left the painting, the one with the square at the end of the red tunnel, the one called *OUT*, at Omar's house, that night, months ago now, the wet and windy day she had taken it to her dealer, in Shoreditch, only to find the window dark, the walls empty, the gallery closed. She had stood on the pavement that day, in the rain, with the painting, thirty-eight years old, childless, divorced, and now, also, officially, career-less. Moneyless. Poor.

She had, still carrying the canvas, passed a different gallery then, around the corner. Billie Jean's.

Billie Jean, who tonight, at Aatifa's wintertime counter, is further away than Marly-Gomont or even Addis, but who, then, that rainy autumn day, being a recovering addict herself, had both shared at the Whitechapel Day Centre meeting, and had a successful show of her paintings in the thriving gallery in Shoreditch, just around the corner from Nouche's, which was dead.

Tonight, Billie Jean is remote, a shadow, distantly involved in the project Omar and Nouche are working on, the spoken word performance, next month, for the Day Centre birthday bash. The poem, *IN,* the painting, *OUT.*

The notebook is still on the table. Omar's lines now lie out in the open, exposed under the neon fixture. It doesn't matter, one way or the other: he knows them by heart. He dries the dishes, as Nouche washes, and his mother stirs. He's not sure Nouche gets the poem. He doesn't know. The piece itself reflects a tunnel, the one he *does* know, the one he traversed, his own WAY OUT. Out of one life, which was dead, the one spent under the needle tree, the Tree of Death--

and into the next, which is here, tonight, beside these two women in the Tower Hamlets kitchen. The way *in*.

Does she get that? Does she get this, that he is loving her, he is half mad with desire; with gratitude, just to be happening beside her?
And that *this* is the way in?

And if not, if she doesn't get it--is this, what he feels for her, still happening?

He doesn't know. He has no answers, just the dish cloth, which he uses, serving them both--that, and the sense, in his chest, that this is his life, this is the way in; this is faith. The faith of his childhood. That *this is it*--it's what Rumi was on about. The God thing.

Billie Jean, tonight, is remote, a distant chink in the Day Centre project, involved with the council, with funding the video, the *cameras, lights,* Nouche had been conjuring up as Omar recited his poem at the kitchen table in the dark. Now, at the counter, it is Aatifa who transports Nouche back to the City of Lights.

To Aatifa, in ways unfathomable even to her, there is no in-between. There are the concourses she carried Omar across on her hip, the shiny floors. There are the North African palaces her family were invited into, the packed mud walls reaching straight for the sky, a setting sun slanting in through a port hole high up in a crest, the air descending warm and gold like honey in the coolness below.

To hear Aatifa speak, tonight, there has never been anything in the world, but elegance, and grace. Anything else is, like Schrödinger's cat, in the eye of the beholder, a mere question of perspective--a lapse in observation.

Omar has not seen his taut, intense girlfriend this loose, this happy, in weeks. She has returned to the table, her legs pulled up under her, her small feet, her pearly toes, bare in their stockings.

She listens, as Aatifa is describing the Dubai Zoo, little Omar climbing in and out of the seat of the red toy car, Aatifa watching from an air-conditioned shelter; Nouche listens as Aatifa moves on to a banquet in the Dubai hotel, skipping gaily to dances in Asmara, the women in their robes moving across the floor like pieces on a chess board under the white, modernist trellis, the Italian palisades, out under the stars.

Music and lights, he thinks, folding both women into the warmth, the light, the happy rhythm of his chest.

Nouche had been happy, and loose, that rainy, windy August night. She'd been drunk. She'd stretched out on her black sheets. She'd been feeling Omar, in the hard-bodied arms reaching under her, with exhilarating power, lifting her from the bed. Her feet were slung over the straight shoulders before her.

Omar, right then, was seeing her. He saw her red passage, glossy like the tunnel, the painting, left by Nouche earlier that evening against his own kitchen counter. He was burning up, his desire for her, his own girlfriend, making him insane. He was having visions, all of her, and of her legs slung over his shoulders, his hands under her, pulling her in: the only way out. He came, shamefully, not even imagining his own triumph--but hers, her long, lithe-limbed, languid contractions.

Music and lights.

The next morning had been equally rainy. Omar had stood in his kitchen at nine, sliding away from the fridge door the painting, wrapped in plastic, still wet from its trip all over Shoreditch, from one gallery to the next, the day before. This was an abysmal autumn, a BBC weather voice had announced, as Omar stood on the tiles, staring at the open fridge. It had been the holy month of Ramadan, still, and he had slept soundly, of course, again, all through dawn. Verily, Omar had thought, staring at a tray of raw steak, left by Nouche the night before, There is a blessing in Sahur.

The night before. Nouche had lain on her black sheets, looking down the mounds of her breasts, down her own creamy belly, to the smooth, silvery crest below. At the shoulders before her, the strong, toned arms. Billie Jean was holding her up with one arm, the other inside her.

Billie Jean is clean, and, unlike Nouche, stone cold sober. She has no excuse. Doesn't need one. This is her thing, the one place where she cannot, and will not, hold back. She suffers the disgrace of being here, at all, not just in the room, but on the planet. Being here, with all her brain cells intact, all her nerve ends zinging. She bears it and grins.

Billie Jean takes each fresh day on the jaw, minute by goddamn minute, breath after fucking breath. She will not go back to anaesthetics, not to heroin, not to crack: she chooses to be *here*, if it kills her.

It is this determination, this lion-heartedness, that Nouche, looking down her own legs, is giving in to, this fearlessness, this *choice*. Nouche wants it, all of it, yielding in radiant waves to the great cat before her. Billie Jean, she thinks, is raw, all there. *Just like Omar.*

If Omar is clasping himself in both hands, seeing Nouche, her open legs, her lazy, luminous glow, at this particular moment, and Nouche, under Billie Jean, is mouthing, *Omar*--what, of all this, in Schrödinger's terms, is actually *happening*?

Aatifa would insist on grace. On elegance. She, tonight, this dark, winter-time evening, insists on the City of Lights. It is global, Aatifa's city, boundless, stretching from Addis to Dubai, from Mecca to Asmara. It includes Marly-Gomont, and lights up even the Tower Hamlets estate. It is radiant, like the stockinged, smiling woman at her table, not quite a daughter, perhaps, but here, tonight, happening, to her son.

Both, Omar and Nouche, that earlier, autumn night, had looked down their own bodies, had stared down, shuddering, at themselves, thinking, *fucking hell.* Both had been happy, shattered, grateful, appalled. Alive.

It was the next morning, that the rest had kicked in, all this, the weather, the rain, the wind, the painting, still bubble wrapped in Omar's arms, as he carried it up the stairs, the dark, dusty Brick Lane staircase opposite the mosque. She'd left it in his kitchen, the night before, drunk, dismal. He'd promised to take it around.

Here he was, key in hand, grateful to be of use. He fiddled with the door, which was open, unlocked. He picked up the canvas, nine months clean and sober, prepared to take life on life's terms if it killed him. His determination had matched Billie Jean's, still sleeping, bone by bone, by bone. Omar walked in the room, carrying the painting, the red passage, the *WAY OUT*, before him-- determined to be alive, to be here now, to be *in*.

8

islands

There is not a decent version of *Islands in the Stream* online. This song, which by all rights, should be soothing Omar's nerves, is, in every version he gets on YouTube, making him insane. He once constructed a tree out of used needles, lived on little but rocks and gear for seventeen years. Still, crack is nothing, he feels today, compared to what Kenny Loggins did to this blinding tune.

Here is Omar, in the Whitechapel Day Centre, gritting his teeth through the demo version, by the BeeGees, the seventies pop group who originally wrote the song.

Islands in the Stream
That is what we are
No one in between
How can we be wrong

Sail away with me
To another world..

Billie Jean, meanwhile, is miming something altogether different.

Something something, she is saying.

Omar stares at her lips moving across the table. Here, inside his own head, she is soundless. All he hears, on repeat, is Barry Gibb and *Islands*. Omar loaded the tune on his phone this morning, and has been listening all through the meeting, from the minute Billie Jean walked into the Whitechapel Day Centre room.

Billie Jean is a recovering addict herself, a few years into the program. She is here to support the event the centre is putting on next month. Billie Jean is speaking, across the round table of the assembly room, to a middle-aged West-Indian from the Tower Hamlets borough, who is wearing a hot pink skirt suit.

'Well,' the woman answers. 'We'd give you money.'

She smiles. Her eyes are laughing, leaving her face smooth as chocolate parfait. Like Omar's mother, Aatifa, who shares this plump, glowing skin.

Money.
It is the only answer, it seems, at this point, to the questions before them.

Right, Billie Jean says. She is wearing a black t-shirt and jeans. Her hair is chopped short to frame her delicate face. She looks relieved.

'Err,' she says. '..How much?'

The woman laughs again. Anwar and Terry, who came into the program with Omar eleven months ago, are smiling, awkwardly, too. Even Chris, their Day Centre counsellor, is wearing a grin.

'Tower Hamlets burough will,' the woman says, 'look at your proposal, and your budget. I understand you want us to fund a recording..'

'Yes,' Chris says.

'Of the.. performances,' the woman says.

'Yeah,' says Billie Jean. Everyone, apart from Omar, nods. They all look up at him and, quickly, he bows in turn.

Omar has not a clue what he is assenting to. Of course, he's aware of the meeting, the council lady, who looks like his mother. He knows why he's here. The birthday party, next month. His own spoken word performance. The poem.

The thought of Nouche makes him flinch. Anger, fear: he doesn't want to know. It makes him mute, and deaf, determinedly so, at this particular moment. He knows, in a general sort of way, what he's here for. Omar nods, wordless, at the meeting, the council woman, Billie Jean: still plugged into his phone, still listening to Barry Gibb, still listening to *Islands in the Stream.*

That is what we are
No one in between

Billie Jean. She should be dead, he thinks, or cowering, hiding away somewhere, in terror. Instead, here she is, across the table, in a plain view.

Outside it rains. It is November. With the winter clock, a chill has fallen over the city. The air seems to have grown fangs, despite the rain. Cold bit at Omar, the moment he left his flat this morning. Even huddled in a wool jumper here, glowering in his seat opposite Billie Jean, he is shivering. He wonders if the shudder, which he seems to feel in his very marrow, may be somehow encoded in his genes. Is the cold, the tremor, simply in his bones?

There she sits, Billie Jean, skinny legs stretched out before her, toned shoulders, bare arms slung on the table, fiercer, more manly somehow, than Omar himself. He could drink her blood.

Sail away with me
To another world

He has Barry Gibb, and the BeeGees, to thank, he supposes, for being here in any capacity at all. He has not walked out, has not pulled Billie Jean across the table. He has not slammed her down the Whitechapel Day Centre concrete stairs.

Omar is here. Present. Sort of. If, to all practical purposes, mute, and deaf, to the meeting, to his peers, to Anwar, Terry, all, like Omar, eleven months into the program, this week. Like him, they're here to plan this, their first birthday, next month, that magical, monstrous hallmark.
One year clean.

Omar is deaf, particularly, specifically--spectacularly, he thinks--to Billie Jean, who, four years clean and a painter herself, is here to help them set up the bash, lending financial muscle by offering one of her works up for auction.

Omar sits glaring, in his earphones, deaf, mute--letting Barry Gibb, of the BeeGees, do the talking, for now.

You do something to me
That I can't explain

Omar had left Nouche, last week, between the black walls of her apartment. They had just then visited his mother, Aatifa, in her Tower Hamlets flat. Omar had watched the two women, that evening, his mother and his French girlfriend, side by side, at Aatifa's council kitchen counter: his mother in her stiff white robe, Nouche in silk and heels.

Nouche will have been divorced from her Paris TV host ex-husband, Alain Mouille, for two years next month. Nouche still carries, even there in Aatifa's kitchen, in her shoulders, in the angle of her chin, of her hair, some spark, some reflection, of the chandeliers, the cascading armatures, the studio lights she's been accustomed to.

Omar's mother, Aatifa, too, has grown up beautiful, a fact not only apparent, that night, in her dark face, but from the glow, the lustre, of her stories. Aatifa had married Omar's diplomat father at thirteen. Taking little Omar to Mecca in the seventies, she had not, as, then, any young Eritrean mother might have done, simply sailed him across the Red Sea. Aatifa had flown the child to Mecca, not just from Addis or Asmara, but from across the continent, from the airports, the royal concourses popping up around the Gulf of Oman like desert diamonds, like jewels in the crown of Arabia; from Dubai, and Qatar.

Here, last week, they had been in Aatifa's wintry, Tower Hamlets kitchen together. Nouche, Omar, his mother. Omar had watched the women at the counter, under the bleak neon buzz. Aatifa, chopping onions, Nouche extinguishing a half-smoked Gaulloise under the tap. Aatifa passing on the cleaver, and Nouche, her small, silk back beside Aatifa's, taking it and running the blade under the tap. Slipping his mother's ancient knife, without thinking, in the drying rack on the counter.

The women, backs turned, had seemed somehow connected, to each other, to the knife, to the act of paring down, of clipping away at dead bits. To the act of cutting themselves out of corners, of pruning, of cutting back themselves, their own lives.

He had looked from his mother, her neck lined in the unkind light, to his girlfriend. Nouche had seemed somehow translucent, as sheer, he had thought, as her stockings, her pearly feet in their heels. For some reason, he'd had a sudden vision, then, of Nouche, months earlier, carrying a painting, up and down the East End.

He'd seen her before him, that autumn day, tottering to her dealer in Shoreditch, who'd had, as it turned out, closed shop. She'd stood before the dark window of her gallery, the bare, blind walls. She'd peered in the dark, staring into the tunnel of the empty shop: the dead end, Omar supposes, of her own career.

He thinks of her in his mother's kitchen, just last week. Back turned, running the blade under the tap, and laying it in the rack.
She frightens him.

His mother's battered cleaver frightens him. Swerving across the kitchen counter in Nouche's pale wrist. The two women scare him, side by side, under the neon light, their lives stripped down to knuckles and bones. He wonders what's left for them to clip at, what, next, will have to go.

Whatever it is they dream of still, whatever it is they may need, Omar thinks, he has not a hope in hell of providing--hanging on here by a thread himself, hanging on to the meeting, to the Whitechapel Day Centre, to *Islands in the Stream*.

The council woman's hot pink nails scrape across the table as she returns a print of one of Billie Jean's paintings.

'We appreciate your contribution,' she says. 'I understand auctioning your

work may attract quite a bit of attention.'
Billie Jean shrugs.

'And fetch a nice sum,' the lady adds.'

'Anything..' Billie Jean grins.

The council woman nods. '..To keep this lot off the street,' she says. 'Or,' she corrects herself, 'to keep our children *in* the street..'

'But not *out* of it,' Terry cuts in, drumming on the table. He raps.

Keep em in-na street

Billie Jean joins in, *But not skagged up to the eye balls*

In-na street, Terry picks up again, *but not Bang*

At-it, like we was.

The deafness is a mercy Omar, meanwhile, is thinking, staring still at Billie Jean. He wonders why he can kill her voice but not her face. How can it be so easy to turn the BeeGees full blast on the phone and blot out sound--yet impossible to simply stare Bille Jean out of her seat, to stare her into extinction? Why is it beyond him to, even, just look away?

Tender love is blind, Barry Gibb sings.

It requires a dedication

Last week, after dinner in Aatifa's winter clock kitchen, Omar had dropped Nouche off at her own apartment, across from the mosque on Brick Lane. He had watched her pick her way across a pool of vomit in her heels, between two restaurant doors, to unlock her own, and go up the stairs in the dark.

Omar had walked home in the cold to his own council flat, toward Whitechapel, leaving behind the brawl of Brick Lane, to traverse the silent, deserted night of the Hanbury Street estates.

Islands in the Stream
That is what we are

'We got rap,' the council woman smiles. 'Obviously.'

Terry grins.

'Your budget includes recording,' the woman continues. Chris, the Day Centre counsellor, nods. 'We got rap,' he says, 'and Spoken Word.'

Everyone looks up at Omar.

Omar, meanwhile, is still musing. Verily, he thinks, there is a blessing in deafness. Unlike *mute*ness, which is potentially disastrous: considering he is here to talk. About speech itself, as it happens. He feels, still plugged into the phone, the stares, from Chris, from the council woman, the one who looks like his mother. She is here, he thinks, to hear him *speak*.

You do something that I can't explain
Hold me closer
And I feel no pain

He doubts, somehow, he can let Barry Gibb do the talking *now*.

No. He needs to man up, get a grip. He is getting looks, too, from Anwar--and from Terry, which is worse as Terry, 'the Cunt', is not known for either his social skills or his gentle, constructive criticism. Not that Omar can be sure, from his sideways vision, that either Anwar or Terry are actually looking at him, as Omar's own eyes are still glued, mutely, murderously, to Billie Jean.

We rely on each other; ah-ah
From one lover to another; ah-ah

Omar has, finally, stopped shivering in the cold, and is now suddenly sweating.
Allah.
It's not like good, wholesome warmth has enveloped him at last, either; it's cold
sweat he feels trickling down his jumper, the foul, stinking kind.
He is going to have to look away: look somewhere else. Sometime. Soon.

Also, more pressingly, he is going to have to unplug his ears, and cut this
lifeline, the one to Barry Gibb, which, he realises with rising dread, is
impossible: which he, at this point, is physically incapable of.

Baby when I met you
There was peace unknown

Omar is no more able to pull the plug on Barry than he is able to either sit here
in the meeting, alone, without the music--or to take his eyes off Billie Jean.

She glances up, straight faced. Billie Jean is lounging in her seat, her shoulders
leaning back, her bare, muscled arms slung unapologetically on the table.
She could be pretty, Omar agonises, if she'd *apply* herself at all. Instead, here
she sits, gazing back, raw, open, a hint of a smile, or a snarl, on her lips. He
feels not a shred of desire, could not get it up to save his life. Women, Omar
despairs, should not *be* like Billie Jean.

The tune, the song, meanwhile, *Islands*, flows along, like the words, the stream
of its title. It is balm. It is honey. He can't explain. All he knows is he needs to
hear it, constantly, on repeat, on his earphones.

I can't live without you if the love was gone
Everything is nothing when you got no one

All he knows: he can't unplug.

He wishes for the melody to drift free somehow, free from the Gibb brothers, free from the backing track. To sit here alone with him in the dark.

Floating there, in Omar's mind, just under the surface, is a different vision of Nouche, of around the same time as the closed down gallery, last autumn: a different memory. It glowers in the dark, on and off, half hidden away. Not that windy, rainy day, on the pavement, with the painting, but the next. The next morning, when it was Omar's turn to carry the painting up and down the East End. Here it flares up again, the memory: His girlfriend, asleep still, at noon. Billie Jean's square arms framing her like a trinket. She glowers, in the centre, Nouche, like a gemstone, in his mind's eye, then fades away into the frame, Billie Jean's embrace, which in turn fades to black.

Omar sits fixed to the Day Centre chair. There is nowhere to go, he panics, nothing to do, but sit here, mute, and wait for the ground to start giving way, for shit to start, seriously, coming down. He doesn't know what he fears more, Terry, and his comments; or his mother, oops, the council woman, and her withering look.

Or himself, reaching across the table, and disemboweling Billie Jean. Knocking her down the concrete stairway, step by fucking step.

It is later, that afternoon, that he is alone, at last. The meeting is over. *Islands* is not. Omar walks home, to his flat, the song still playing. He walks the Tower Hamlets pavement, which is cracked, and dirty, and littered. He doesn't know. What he's doing. Where he's going. Home.

What does that even mean, after seventeen years of being out here in the wintry chill, of living on the streets? What does it mean, to walk home today, clean, sober, saved, more or less--no blood on his hands, no guts, no one left for dead, at the table; not much harm done, altogether. He has not managed to talk, has sat through the meeting silent, exchanging looks with Chris. Omar kept still, right through to the end, a rock in the flow, in the stream. Now he's walking home.

It is cold. His sweat has long dried to a stench, and now just leaves him feeling foul. He walks, passing the corners he knows so well, each bearing the imprint of some transaction, some crime; some transgression.

Baby when I met you

He left her on her stairs, again, last night, his girlfriend. He doesn't know where *she* is, either. Home, he supposes. Her home. Though god knows what that might mean to Nouche, who used that term for *Maison* Mouille, her ex-husband's 5th arrondissement residence; for their eighteenth century windows, overlooking the Quartier, the Boulevard; for their *Saint-Michel* double doors.

Home. He is headed there, himself, his home, the council flat he was allocated five months ago, and which is still bare save the table in the lounge, two straight-backed chairs, and the painting, left there months earlier, by Nouche.

He doesn't know where Nouche is this afternoon, hasn't seen her since last night. Is she happy? He doesn't know. Is she sad? Depressed? He doesn't know that, either. He may add the questions to a long list of things he has no way, today, of knowing, of even guessing at.
Is she safe?

He thinks of the canvas, the red tunnel marked *WAY OUT*, stacked, still, against the wall of his flat. Again, he sees her wandering around Shoreditch with it, that day, in the wind and the rain. She is broke, he knows that much. She's a painter, and she's not selling, she is not, currently, even showing.

It is Billie Jean, he thinks, passing the tower estate on the corner of Hanbury street, Billie Jean who has been sipping orange juice at openings, *her* openings, one of which was on the eighth floor of this very building.
Omar glances up. It's a place he might have called home, as it happens, at some

point in the skag-ridden seventeen years he spent before meeting Nouche--as
Omar, years ago, used to live on one of these crack house floors himself.
He looks up the grim stack of concrete balconies. This is the place, he thinks,
where he'd pass out under the Tree of Death.

Home.

There will be no welcome mat waiting, when he gets home today, in the new,
council flat. No mail, no messages. This is it.

Islands in the stream

He walks the November streets, thinking of his girlfriend. Is she safe? Again
she flares up in his mind, a gemstone, set in a frame he does not wish to dwell
on, a frame instantly blacked out, replaced by wind and rain, as he pictures her
walking away from her gallery, stooped under the *WAY OUT* canvas, drizzle
blowing in her face.

Is she even *here*? Omar thinks, walking home today--Is she even planning to be
here tomorrow, to stick around?
Or is she planning a way out of her own?

Again he wonders which part of her life may have to go, next, what is left for
her to cut away at. He thinks of her face, her dark hair, her brooding lips, and
knows he doesn't know.
He knows nothing.

That is what we are
No one in between
How can we be wrong

What he knows, is that he needs the brothers Gibb to keep singing.

We ride it together, ah-ah
Making love with each other, ah-ah

Again, she flares up, centre stage, Nouche: crystalline, and red, like cut amber, framed by the darkness at the edge of Omar's own mind. He had walked up her dim stairs, that August morning, the painting before him.

He'd stepped in, among her black walls. The blinds had been drawn. Light streaked onto the bed. She slept, lips parted. Cheek resting in the cup of that straight, toned shoulder. His key in the lock, his feet on the boards, did not as much as wake them.

He'd stood in the room.

Billie Jean's black, skinny jeans, her phone, lay on the chair. Her wallet on the table.

Her hard body folded around Nouche, who shone in the slanted light.

He'd left. This is what he can't get past. Before he knew it, he'd backed out. Stood out in the hallway.

No. That's not what kills him. He'd gone *back*.

Does she know?

That he turned on the doorstep, and crept back in, to pick up the canvas, and carry it back, all the way, carry it past the silent Hanbury street estates, under the concrete crack house tower, the Tree of Death? Home?

He doesn't know. He doesn't know a thing.

What he needs, right now, pacing home from the Whitechapel Day Centre, is the song, *Islands in the Stream*.

He needs it alone, just the words, and the melody: loose, single notes, scattered downstream. Floating away, naked, bare. Just the essence, the balm. No explanation. Just this. Going home. The song, and the empty Tower Hamlets streets. The cold, and the dark.

Later, that evening, it's her, on the phone, and later, still, it's her at his door.

They sit at the table, in Omar's bare room, on the straight-backed chairs. He hands her a mug. Tea. She looks, he thinks, slightly drunk. He is unsure.

It's his first birthday, next month, one year clean and sober, his first year, in seventeen, of wearing clothes, of sleeping in a bed. His first year, next month, with her.

She has not, over the past year, grown to him familiar. She is not somebody he knows.

Does she know? Does she know he knows?

Across the room, the painting still sits against the wall. Even last week, in his mother's kitchen, he had recited to her, by heart, the poem he'd written.

WAY OUT, he'd whispered,

Is spelled Backwards
WAY IN

Does she know he'd crept back, into the room, past the chair, the jeans, the wallet on the table, to pick up the canvas? That he'd backed out, again, carrying the painting under the tower, home?

Nouche sets down the mug. She leans across Omar's table, her wine-breath in his face, sharp like crack, like the floor he used to wake on, under the Tree of

Death.

He stares at her. What could have possessed him to go *back*? Even he doesn't understand. He understands nothing. Nouche leans over to kiss him. Omar closes his eyes. She's an island. A place he doesn't know.

It is not until he opens his mouth, his own lips, to meet hers, that he knows *this*: this stream, this aliveness--this other thing. That he knows what he *does* know.

9

lights

Camera, lights. *Rolling*.

Nouche watches from the middle. The Day Centre Auditorium is a madhouse. Billie Jean is shooting. Omar is on stage. Terry has gone awol. Boy George hovers in the wings.

It is December, at last, Christmas lights flickering all over Whitechapel. Outside, the shop fronts present a unified, if epileptic, take on this Christian affair. Tinsel trees bloom in their halal doorways, rainbow fairy lights flash in mad, syncopated unison.

It's the birthday bash. Not just Our Lord Christ's--but this lot's. Marquis, Anwar, Omar, the Whitechapel Day Centre peer group. They're one year clean.

In the Auditorium, steam rises from the crowd. Drums roll from the decks. The strobe fires, phased to the grimy beat. Marquis, lithe, grimly handsome, clutches a headphone to his shoulder, as he drops in a deep, rolling bass. The floor groans. Dancers, hoods pulled over their faces, bob to the bass and light, as if caught in their slipstream.

These boys have sold crack to school kids. They mugged young mothers, robbed corner stores, have stolen everything from Mercedes to pushchairs. Marquis himself got fucked up the ass just up the road in Dalston more times than even Boy George. He throws another plate on, spins it back, one ear on the vinyl, one ear on the floor, holds the record in place, then, as he counts, over the bobbing hoods, lets it rip.

Deeper, the crowd is sinking, deeper in sync, deeper in all of this, the sweat, the music, the strobe. Lights.

Omar waits on stage. Terry, their rapper, was meant to go on first, before Omar. Terry needed these firecracker beats, whereas Omar, for his own Spoken Word thing, could do with something a bit less hectic. He's about to recite poetry, he thinks, not to incite the crowd to burn down every Christmas tree on Whitechapel High Street.

From below, Nouche watches the confusion. Her painting, the red tunnel with the square at the heart, hangs centre-stage. It's beautifully lit. She follows as Billie Jean's camera pans the stage set, passing over Omar's tall shape, and zooming on the painting, which flares up and disappears back into the night in the strobes, flashing on and off, like a secret exit, a gateway into another world.

In the Auditorium, Billie Jean pans out over the crowd, which is kicking up a sweat. She rolls along the floor, where black hoods ride Marquis' wave under the strobes, like a ballet of mobster monks, a Trappist gangster troupe.

Where is Terry, their rapper? God only knows. Nouche, meanwhile, watching the cola-fuelled mob, could use a drink. This whole clean and sober dancing business is deep and dark. Freaky.

It's been a year today for Omar. A year since he woke, on a concrete parking lot somewhere, the Whitechapel Sainsbury's, possibly, he'd been thinking--only to find it was dark, dusk. His eyelids crackled with the frost. He'd sat up, and the notion had occurred that it was Christmas Eve. That he was freezing up from the *in*side, his teeth clattering all the way from his marrow, which was cringing, crimping. Then, that this stop-freeze feeling, did not stop with him, Omar, but that he seemed to spread it out, that the whole world was contaminated, implicated, shutting down in turn. Low-level frenzy, desperation, was in the air. The world of traffic, of exchange, was grinding to a halt. He jumped to his feet, his bones crunching under him, and bolted for the the supermarket entrance, the bright doors in the distance, where, just as he arrived, the fat guard was turning his back.
This was a bit of luck, as Omar was barred from Sainsbury's. He'd been chased from every shop he knew in Tower Hamlets, even from churches, surgeries and homeless shelters.
Omar tried the glass doors, which yielded to his touch. *Bismillah*.
The prospect of spending yet another holy night without money, food or dope had been narrowly avoided.

He leaned against the glass, pushing in his full weight. Just then, the guard turned around. Omar froze. The guard peered at Omar, and smiled.
Omar, by now, really could not believe his luck. There must be a God, after all. A new guard. Of course. Christmas Eve. Bismillah. Temps.
Omar smiled back, and, casually, reached again for the glass.
The guard, still smiling, lifted one palm, buttressing the door. *Closing,* he mouthed. *No one in.*

From the awning, the parking lot, as it started to snow, Omar watched the customers still idling down the aisles, piling up turkey at the checkouts. Not that he cared about food, but stealing was his single marketable skill, and he was clucking. He'd been awake barely three minutes. He was feeling sick, already, convulsions jolting his joints, with not seconds, not minutes, not even hours to get through, but three fucking infidel days.

That's when he sank back down to the concrete ground. *Allah.*
Please, he thought. Just get this over with.
He sat on the ground as the parking lot emptied out, with a crushing sense of deja vu, of having seen this all before, many more times than he could, or cared to, remember. Another festive season hitting at the very last minute, with its endlessness, its deprivation.
Allah, he thought, Just make this end. Please.
Never again, he prayed, as he sat in the parking lot with nothing, no hope, just carols and tinsel and lights in the dark, all around, stars in the street.

It was later, that same Christmas week, that Nouche had been in front of the mosque in Brick Lane, prodding the lock of her bike with a knife. She'd been divorced a year then. A year since she'd left Maison Mouille, the Quartier, the street lanterns glittering off her antique windows on Boulevard Saint-Michel. She'd fumbled in the dark, in the grimy East End chill, over the bike, her fingers rigid with cold. The lock was frozen shut. In the light from the mosque's doorway, she'd pried at it with her father's pocket knife, the old French farmer's knife she'd carried with her all the way from Marly-Gomont. An ageing man, just then exiting the Brick Lane mosque, had gently taken the blade from her hands.

She'd watched, in the falling snow, how at last the bike had been locked to the fence. Going up her stairs in the dark, she'd prayed the slippered men, creeping in and out of the mosque all through the night, would somehow watch over it, save her bike from the freezing, starving Brick Lane night.

She'd ended up watching over the street herself, that night, watching the men in the soft light from the mosque, from her own dark window. Knife in hand. It sat in her palm, as snow covered over the tracks on the road, the footsteps coming and going from the old chipped doors. She'd thought of her old Saint Michel view, the 5th arrondisement at her doorstep. Mouille, who'd taken her from the one-street hamlet of Marly-Gomont, to the chandeliers, the spotlights, of the *Soiree* studio.

She remembered the Christmas fetes they'd thrown, the food, the guests, the stars. Lagerfeld, Deneuve, Huppert, she remembers being cornered by Kristen Scott Thomas and her impeccable French. The unimaginable Sophia Loren, who'd made Nouche, whose posture is straight from Degas, feel like a piglet. Laughing in the wings with Charlotte Gainsbourg, just a few years younger than Nouche, both giddy with sudden clumsiness and awe.

That Brick Lane night though, last Christmas, Nouche had found herself, finally, in the bath. Her legs silvery in the pink water, the whole tub cupped inside the black walls of her bathroom. She'd lain in the middle, swaddled in steam and tuberose. The grip of the knife slowly flicking in one pale wrist; the blade scraping away at the other.

***

Tonight, in the Whitechapel Auditorium, Nouche watches from below, as Billie Jean records. Marquis phases the entire scene from the decks, thunder and strobe lights, like Thor wielding his hammer from the stage. Omar has climbed down, and is now in the crowd, his long limbs both solid and loose, like lava, bubbling, evenly, in sync with the floor, with the night. The stage is bare, apart from the strobes, the painting: the unearthly passage, flickering away.

Anwar, a tall, baby-faced man with a pouch, is gesturing over the din, to Chris, the Day Centre counsellor. Their rapper, Terry, is still missing. Billie Jean, from behind the camera, seems to be signalling to Chris, while talking, simultaneously, on her phone. Boy George. He is on the other side of the stage, nodding into his own phone. Nouche has met him, too, on set, at *Soiree*, she suddenly realises, although she doubts he would remember.

It's Billie Jean, it appears, who brought Boy George. She talks into the phone, without taking the camera off the crowd, registering the mayhem around her with a slow, steady pan.

Apart from Billie Jean's lens, the only thing on the itinerary running smoothly, on track, just as planned, is the crowd. Omar's lot sure have pulled in the punters tonight. The Day Centre Auditorium is packed. God knows where these kids have come from, but the austerity-plagued council of Tower Hamlets, who bankrolled the evening in hopes of promoting drugs-free street culture, must be pleased; they're getting value for money.

Marquis, of course, was once a dub-step DJ packing clubs from Goa to Berlin, before ending up in a crack house, renting out his arse in Dalston. It's Anwar though, soft, pudgy Anwar, who's about to shift the whole thing, the whole night, into a different gear.

Anwar had come in a year ago, violent, obese, mute. He'd opened his mouth to speak only months later, after weeks in detox, after months of counselling sessions and, upstairs in the conference room, Whitechapel Day Centre meetings. It's Omar, who remembers. *I am more*, Anwar had whispered in the silent meeting room at last ..*Than the child of warring parents*.

Now Anwar's gesturing over the din, still, to Chris. Billie Jean cuts to Marquis, the Norse God conductor. The Auditorium shakes. She rotates around the room, over the dancers, who flash in the light, past Omar, the moving volcano, whose solid shoulders seem to smoulder in the dark. Billie Jean pans across the floor, to Nouche. In the shade, in cream silk, Nouche's small, straight body is sharp as a cut out. Then, with each flare of the strobe, she catches fire, the fine, pleated dress glowering like skin.

On her end of the lens, Nouche holds her breath. To her right, Omar's height, his bubbling, lava shape, projects from the crowd. Left, Billie Jean, bare-armed behind the camera, is a cannon, terse as string in black jeans and sneakers. She zooms in on Nouche, who is burning a tiny, syncopated, hourglass figure in the viewer.

Billie Jean. Is she her lover?
Nouche doesn't know.

Billie Jean wields the lens, like a ray gun, fixing Nouche in her gaze. Nouche dances, the pearly dress clinging to her body.

***

Now remember that Christmas week, a year earlier, when Nouche had been struggling with her bike. The next morning she descended her stairs. She stepped out in the street, where a drizzly rain had washed away the snow. Omar, by this time, had just spent three days on the Whitechapel Detox ward. He'd been shattered, insane, but somehow, madly, alive. Reborn. *Allah*.

Omar had come out to pray. That is not how Nouche had found him, though, that morning. Omar had entered the Brick Lane mosque in a clean white shirt, only to be thrown out, minutes later, by the same old man who had so kindly locked her bike to the fence the night before. The same old man, who had routinely chased Omar off the premises for the past seventeen years.

Omar sat on the steps of the mosque, in the rain, and the clean shirt, as Nouche stepped from her doorway to unlock her bike. There is something, she remembers thinking, crossing the road. Something about him.
Her bike'd been gone.

Back to the booming Auditorium. She remembers the thought. *Something*, she thinks, now, a year later, dancing across from her boyfriend. Still.
There is something, still, about him.

She remembers thinking it the first time, remembers the rain, the shirt.
Most, she remembers her buzzer, at dusk, later that same December day. She
remembers parting the curtain, and lifting the heavy pane, to find Omar,
standing, in the street below. With a bike. Nouche's bike. Omar beaming up at
her.

What she forgets, is the pain shooting up her arm as she had opened that
window.
Omar does not. He remembers. Even here, perhaps, tonight, on the dance floor.
Even as he watches her flare up in Billie Jean's lens. Watches her burn in the
light. Buried deep somewhere in his lava body, there bubbles that memory; the
bandaged wrist.

Chris, meanwhile, gestures to Anwar. He's pointing up. The ceiling? Nouche
wonders, in the thunder from the decks. She sees Anwar agree, and too, lift a
finger to the ceiling, trying to get Omar's attention. *Meeting,* he mouths. *Ad
hoc.* Omar nods back. Chris sticks up both hands in reply, miming, *In ten.*

Never again, Nouche, the butcher, had thought, the year before, that night, in
the bath. She'd watched her body change colour in the tub, her silver limbs
turning rosy with the water. Never ever again.

If she crossed her road the next morning, to cross paths, with a complete
stranger, someone who had not a claim on her in the world, perhaps it was this
thought, *never again,* which had connected some wire, burned some pathway,
and prompted that other thought. Something. *Something about him.*

Under the neon fixtures of the Whitechapel Day Centre meeting room, the floor
softly booms as below, in the Auditorium, Marquis still rules. Here Anwar,
Chris, Billie Jean have taken seats around the conference table. Omar has led
Nouche, too, up the concrete stairs. It is Nouche's first time up here.
..A moment of silence.. Chris is saying, ..For the still suffering addict.

There is not a sound in the room, apart from the buzz of neon, the thud from below. Anwar, Billie Jean, sit with eyes closed. Nouche blinks in the strip lights. When people close their eyes, she notices, the brow becomes the third eye. The window of the soul. Like the spot, the little star, between the eyes, on a Buddha statue.

Omar's dark face, to her right, glows. Traces of thoughts, dreams--something, Nouche thinks--ripple gently, as always, along his forehead. Always something, she thinks.

Across from her, Billie Jean's face is chiseled, unperturbed under her short, dark hair. A slight frown conveys something of her essence, even as she sits here wordless, eyes closed: still proclaims her presence in the room, like a rogue, brooding star of Bethlehem.

It will be Omar's turn, later tonight, to go onstage. He will read a poem called *In*, as the painting, the exit, flashes behind him.

Way Out, he'll read, a low riding dub rhythm backing him up.

..Is Spelled Backwards, he continues.

Baby.

Way Out.. he says, Is Spelled *Way In*.

In. Nouche is *in* the crowd. In the auditorium, in a sweat, in a silk dress, in a dance, in a band of merry fools, of hoodlum Trappists, of reformed addicts and thieves, all stone cold sober, all deeply, darkly, *in* to it; into all this.

Next is Anwar. They've lost their rapper, by then, poor Terry. The cunt. Thank God they've got Boy George, sipping a seven-up, to replace him. It's Anwar though, mute, obese Anwar, who clambers onto the stage now, beside Marquis, who has just stepped up the pitch a notch or so, whipping the diet-coke infused pit back to a frenzy.

Nouche watches from the fringe, with Boy George. He doesn't stand a chance. Anwar is a menace, spray gunning the crowd with verbal rhythm. Spewing it out, insurgency-style, turning Whitechapel into an East End West Bank, a dance hall Jerusalem.

Can't believe.., a girl in a silver mini groans, I'm dancing..
She pants. ..To *Anwar.*

But all that is later. First, Nouche sits in the impromptu meeting. She looks around the table, the closed, silent faces. She wonders what they're doing. What is it this lot does in a meeting? *Pray?*

She thinks of Christmas with Mouille, of La Loren, La petite Gainsbourg. The holly, the game, the wine, the candelabras. The river glittering in the studio windows, the City of Lights.

Perhaps this is where she remembers the wrists. Perhaps not. The moment has passed, anyway, as a great crashing noise shakes the room and Terry tumbles from the door, stumbling over a chair and sitting down in a corner.

No one moves. Silence returns under the neon lights. Nouche continues to watch the faces around the table, their eyes closed, lost in something she cannot fathom. Another crash from the corner, then a carrier bag loudly crackling. More hiss, crack-snap, fizz: plastic foil being torn from something inside Terry's bag, as the concrete floor softly stomps under the table, the lights buzz overhead, deep breathing emanates from the small circle gathered at the centre of the room.

Now a big clatter, as Terry stumbles, again, and dunks onto the table, *thud,* a man-sized carton box. There it sits, like a bomb, ticking away, while Chris scrapes his throat, and Omar, Billie Jean, Anwar, open, finally, their eyes and seem to return to the room.

The box is black, a gold ribbon hastily ripped off. Terry sits slumped in the corner. Billie Jean glowers. Even Omar, pudgy Anwar, radiate gloom.

Chris sits staring ahead, tight-lipped. The floor thumps like a hollow, concrete heartbeat.

It is Nouche, the carnivore, at last, who cuts through the air of woe. Who flicks a pale wrist.

Is this where she remembers? The bath, the blade? Who knows.
Maybe, sitting here, between two lovers, she remembers that other night. Moon dancing for Billie Jean.

Are they lovers? Not since.

Billie Jean had been waiting for her, by her door, that autumn night, waiting to lead her upstairs. All she herself had done, Nouche thinks, was dance.

As she's done this evening, the lens zooming in on her, as she will do later tonight, at midnight, when Anwar, who sits here in the meeting still a war child, a boy, will open his mouth, and become the man of the hour. When Nouche's tight little shape will again burn a figure eight before the camera, *Music and Lights*, on the dance floor.

Does Omar know?

Nouche doesn't know. Can he tell?

Terry's black box still ticks on the table. What Nouche doesn't know, is that whatever Omar knows, or doesn't know, *he* will not forget the bandage. Omar remembers.

Behind the box, Anwar sits picking mutely at a scab. Billie Jean seems frozen in a glare. Below, a lone raver blows a whistle, a shrill, piercing call, caged in concrete.

It's Nouche's pale wrist, up here, that catches the light, and dances, over the table.

103

It hovers over the box. Her Chanel nails pick an outsized, pearly chocolate. For an instance, it floats there in the air, the white glaze flickering in the neon light. With no stretch of the imagination would Nouche, the butcher, in fact eat this.

She looks around the table. Again, she thinks of Mouille, of the spreads of game, the candles, the wine. Nouche holds up the chocolate, lifting a lazy lash, to Billie Jean, left, then Omar, right.

She would have chosen, she thinks suddenly, neither. It was Omar, a year ago this week, who chose *her*. Who had chased his own thieving lot all across the East End that day, to appear at her door at dusk, bearing the rusty bike.

Next, it had been Billie Jean, who'd been waiting by that same door, one windy night months later. Who had somehow managed, step by lionhearted step, to lead Nouche up her own Brick Lane staircase.

The chocolate still hovers, white between scarlet nails. Nouche again feels her spine tingle, as she remembers the moon dance, undressing between her own black walls. Before Billie Jean.

Slowly, the wrist descends, as Nouche realises it is not the woman, bare armed, across the table, she is in thrall of. It's not the smouldering man either, beside her.

It's the soft spot, Nouche thinks, inside herself--a blood red passage--she can't help but stare at. A gateway. It's not for weak hearted.
Nouche had, she sees now, not even chosen Mouille. It was he, who'd appeared on a Paris platform one day and, in a fit of mad *brille*, slung off his Pierre Cardin jacket. Hurled it to the tiles, right where she stood waiting for the metro, in her heels. Flung it at her feet.

All she does, Nouche realises now, is wait.
The bonbon still hovers, mid-air, over the stomping floor, the gaping box.
The weak heart, Nouche knows, is hers. The choice is not.
She yawns.

It's theirs.

Meanwhile, she's *in*.

She's *in* the meeting. *In* with this band of fools. In, even, with poor Terry, who's passed out in the corner. The cunt.

She places the bonbon before her, on the table. Then she lifts the box, and hands it to Omar.

Below, an entire troupe of ravers--reformed, Nouche supposes--now seems to have landed at the party. At least a dozen whistles shriek with that particular pitch of madness that will cut straight through absolutely anything, even the reinforced ceiling of the Auditorium, the concrete floors of the Whitechapel Detox Centre.

Later that night, Nouche'll be *in* with Anwar, as he climbs his way up the podium, and moans, shouts, bites his way through the most demented bits of Marquis' set. Nouche will be *in* then, even, with the ravers, in their tunics and Dr. Seuss hats, in silver minis and bras, hounding on, toasting, Anwar with their whistles.
She'll be in, finally, that night, with Boy George--who, as she feared, has not the faintest memory of either *Soiree*, her, or entire chunks, for that matter, of the City of Lights, but will dance with her nonetheless. Fat and bald, she'll think, like Father Christmas. Gorgeous. Radiant.

That evening though, up in the conference room, she places the bonbon before her, and waits, the pale glaze sitting under the neon buzz, like a melting dance card.

From Nouche, Omar receives the box. He scans it for fudge, his favourite.
In the corner, with a bolt, Terry wakes. Omar hands the spread to Anwar.
Behind Billie Jean's stony frame, Terry tumbles from his chair. Chomping, Omar glances around the table, where Nouche's confection still sits and waits.

Even Billie Jean, at last, surrenders, and passes on the box, to Chris. Omar snatches up the bonbon.

The Whitechapel Day Centre meeting may begin.